ROGUE'S ATLAS

66 Flash Fiction Stories

Rogue's Atlas: 66 Flash Fiction Stories is published under Reverie, a sectionalized division under Di Angelo Publications, Inc.

Reverie is an imprint of Di Angelo Publications.

Printed in the United States of America.

Di Angelo Publications
4265 San Felipe #1100
Houston, Texas 77027

Library of Congress
Rogue's Atlas: 66 Flash Fiction Stories
ISBN: 978-1-955690-42-3

Words: John Long
Cover Artwork: Samuel Francis
Interior Illustrations: Jason Rowlett
Cover Design: Savina Deianova
Interior Design: Kimberly James
Editors: Cody Wootton, Ashley Crantas, Willy Rowberry

Downloadable via Kindle, Nook, iBooks, and Google Play.

For educational, business, and bulk orders, contact distribution@diangelopublications.com.

1. Fiction --- Action & Adventure
2. Fiction --- Humorous --- General
3. Fiction --- General

ROGUE'S ATLAS

66 Flash Fiction Stories

JOHN LONG

Illustrations by Jason Rowlett

INTRODUCTION
Adventures in Flash

Rogue's Atlas arose from a simple plan: start at Ground Zero, the closest point to detonation. Then shift that point, story to story, to keep the tales flashing within a thousand words or less. With careful distillation of the *vaina*.

In cooking, reducing a liquid means simmering until some of the water evaporates, which intensifies the flavors, thickens the broth, and causes it to take up less volume. Temperature matters, of course.

I think of flash fiction as the purple beads and bits of channeled whelk shell used by the Eastern Woodlands tribes to fashion their strings of wampum, used for storytelling, as ceremonial gifts, and for currency.

—Venice, California
May, 2022

FLASHES

GHOST
TRAIN

TALLY HO!

I woke in a panic. Somehow, between the time I'd passed out and when I came to, my self went missing.

I searched under the bed. Checked my pockets. Rummaged the garage. No self. Maybe my neighbor Leopold had seen something.

I ran out front. It was garbage day. The trashman thrust his head from his truck and yelled, "Hey buddy, you lose your self or something?"

Without a self, I was nothing but rubble, and rubble can't speak.

"I know that look," said the trashman. "I collect the pieces, as needed." He nodded toward the back of his truck, rank as hell's outhouse, compactor pulverizing. "Better talk to Sal, over at the Fun Zone. I'll give him a heads-up."

The Fun Zone was an old amusement park I hadn't visited since grade school. Took me till sunset to find the place. The music had died. The painted horses stood frozen on the carrousel. The Ferris wheel still against gray sky.

One light shone over by The Ghost Train, where I found Sal, who motioned grandly toward an old car. Old as Sal's tailcoat with its fraying gold trim. His scruffy black top hat. I stared at the track running into a dark mountain. I hated these haunted houses.

"It's a cracker jack ride," said Sal. "And most dangerous."

I slithered into the car. A bar fell across my lap. Rusty wheels rasped as I rattled through a portal and into the mountain, creeping past shaded rooms, each featuring scenes from my life that, once upon a time, I'd fought off with dodgeball, Jimi Hendrix, and promising lies. I looked impossibly small in the scenes. And terrified.

I gripped the bar across my waist and clenched my eyes shut.

The car froze, and only crept on when I peeked out at my form, curled into a fetal knot. At my outraged junior high wrestling coach, demanding I explain those welts on my back. Me pleading with him to forget it. Skateboarding through traffic, chancing to get hit. Bivouacking in *Hardy Boys* books.

Other scenes flew at me in a rush. Stealing ice cream from Safeway and getting caught. A report card full of Ds. The shame on Rose's face afterwards. The world, and everyone in it, sidling away.

The car rattled out of the mountain. A quick U-turn, and back to Sal, who bowed at the waist as the car hove to at his feet.

"There's no self in there," I said, blabbing from instinct. "Only a heap of broken pieces. Garbage."

"That's you," said Sal. "That's what you've got to work with."

My fear didn't need a self to talk through.

"No thanks!"

But the bar across my lap wouldn't budge.

"You can't get off the ride until it's over, I'm afraid," said Sal, who I pictured taming lions under The Big Top.

My self was somewhere in that mountain, and ghastly as it felt, I had to reclaim it. I grimaced at the old ringmaster and said, "Let

’er rip.”

Sal tipped his hat and threw the car into gear, and I rolled back into the mountain. Through bright scenes full of made-up friends, all of us carousing. Smashing home runs in Pony League. Homecoming King, the crown sitting crooked on my head. Prizes and commendations. Heaps of money. All the girls. A prom of sunny fantasies within my own dark mountain.

Then another kind of laugh. Uncanny as an evil clown. The lights died out.

The car turned abruptly and shot down an incline, freefalling past room after room as I swelled before my eyes. Snarling and immense, straddling the tracks.

The car shot between the towering legs of a colossus, clattered past other rooms, other scenes, where I drove my fist into somebody’s face. Told a girl I loved her, then chewed through her innocence like potluck ribs. My old Honda Civic, the front end wrapped around a tree, radiator geysering. And me, epically hammered. Ten-Jägermeister-shots-and-three-tabs-of-Adderall-hammered. Violently twisting in the front seat, trying to kick the side window out.

The Ghost Train ground up steep track and across the desert of my fears, where a shell-shocked punk, searching for something holy, tromped past a horse head on the sand. Shielding my eyes. Broadsided by gusts. By everything I’d believed and hoped for, had ever felt, ever done, had ever been. Blowing through me. A soul full of sand, overflowing the rooms and onto the track. Filling the mountain.

I lurched out into night. The car stopped and the bar released me. Sal calmly stepped over, a young woman trembling beside him. I knew her look, and what she was in for.

I stepped clear as the woman, clutching Sal’s gloved hand, lowered into the car. The bar dropped over her waist and she spun toward me, but her mouth could not make words. I had no patch for her havoc. The car trundled off and through the portal.

Something exploded in my chest. I bolted after the car, but Sal grabbed me.

"I'm not done yet!" I said.

"You're never done, my friend," said Sal. "But your ride is over." His hand on my shoulder felt solid.

Behind us, a shriek of grinding metal as the Ferris wheel—recalling how to spin—lurched, stopped, and lurched again. Empty gondolas swaying. The ringmaster smiled, knocked the dust off his top hat, and adjusted it just so on his head. "Tally-ho."

"Tally-ho," I repeated and shuffled off onto the road, streetlights gleaming.

A garbage truck pulled alongside and the trashman peered from the window. "Need a lift?"

I patted myself down. Felt my feet, unsteady on the sidewalk. Glanced behind at the Ferris wheel, turning in fits and starts. The night felt fearsome as the feeling in my chest.

"Think I'm good," I said, waving the trashman on.

Dead reckoning, searching for something holy, I assumed my name and walked into the jeweled night.

SIDE BY SIDE

Late afternoon. Day five. The three of us clawed onto Ship's Prow Ledge, 1,800 feet up the South Face of Mt. Watkins. After hauling up the bags and anchoring off for the night, we sat motionless on the granite portico, hardly talking. Shadows slithered through the valley and up the glassy wall.

Though roped together at the waist, a distance stretched between us, defending our solitude. I felt hollow and remote till remembering Rilke's offering—that if somehow I could love that distance, a piercing intimacy side by side might grow. Then I might see the others, whole against the sky.

I watched Dale fire up the little stove and start boiling some rice. He'd climbed a hundred walls by then, smitten as he was by terra incognito. We all were, but Dale took our collective pipedreams and made them real. Launching up unclimbed monoliths and embracing the unknown with an open heart. He'd study photos of future climbs ("routes"), listening to old Coltrane albums, winding up his mainspring. Then grab a couple of us and we'd chase the route in Dale's mind. We usually found it, too, at the end of our faith and ability—boundary experiences, for us and countless others who would follow. Some frightening battles, but Dale always offered his last sip of water.

Hal, sorting gear, recoiling ropes, taught some sort of science at USC. He could explain anything. I once heard him explain nothing. That's where the climbing came in. "It makes no sense at all," he'd say, which to Hal is what made it so valuable. He'd head up the "Big Lonesome," often with Dale, to frustrate all his knowing. To rekindle his need for mystery. To stoke a passion with the smashing indifference of Nature—which also made no sense. In Hal's overexplained world, what was more precious than the inexplicable?

We ate the rice, exhausted and wordless on Ship's Prow Ledge. And split a can of warm beer, which exploded when Hal pulled the tab, spraying over Dale and him, who I saw for the first time, whole against the sky.

SURFING THE ROOSTER

We met in front of the Grove Theater (featuring *Woodstock: The Movie*), directly across from Miller's Feed Store, a cluttered acre lying in deep shadow. Tina went incognito, skipping the screaming-red lipstick she always wore, even while skateboarding down from Mt. Baldy, say, or torturing Madonna songs.

"In case we get caught," she said, playing dumb for effect. "Otherwise, they'll know."

We jogged across the street and I shook the fence like mad. Everyone feared the man-eating guard dog, which never showed, not even as Tina yelled, "Fiiiidoooo!"

"I knew it was baloney," she chuckled as we slunk around front, where the fence didn't have concertina wire on top. We climbed over and tiptoed to the steel scaffolding that rose like a space needle, topped by a giant fiberglass rooster, rotating in a spotlight—conspicuous mascot for Miller's Feed Store, and an Upland, California, landmark. Damn thing looked almost holy, haloed against the night sky like that.

Tina raced up the rungs and I followed. Fifty feet never felt higher; Miller's Feed and all of Upland spread out below us. We bellycrawled onto the small platform below the rooster. Tina snuggled close, grabbed my hand, and bit it hard.

"I'm scared," she said, thrown open as the Sea of Cortez. I rubbed the purple teeth marks, knowing we could rattle the stars and never die. But we might get into big trouble. Squad cars came and went from police HQ, several blocks over. All the houses dozed several blocks east. But anyone looking up could spot the rooster, and anyone on it, from a mile away. They better.

I grabbed the slick rooster tail and boosted Tina onto a flat spot behind the sloping neck, climbed on board, and shimmied behind her, and we rode the rooster for the required full revolution, the spotlight blinding as the electric motor whinnied and *ca-thunked* from sudden loading. We slid off and raced down the rungs, laughing to keep from exploding.

We spotted the police cruiser—no siren but red light flashing—wheeling up to the drive in front of Miller's Feed, just as we hit the yard.

"Take cover!" said Tina, dropping into a sumo stance and scanning the grounds like Harley Quinn. But the buildings were locked. Same with the trucks all around. The only fence we could climb would land us on top of the squad car.

"The silo!" I said.

We dashed over to a towering grain silo and climbed another ladder, gaining an opening, small as a doghouse door, way up there.

"Crap!" said Tina.

I squeezed alongside her on the ladder and we peered into the silo, packed flush to the opening with stanky feed pellets.

We heard what had to be a cop, clambering over the fence out front.

Tina dove for it. I piled in after and plunged to my chest. We gripped each other's arms, smelly feed up to our chins, gagging on the scratchy duff welling off the pellets.

The merciless itching started on my face, rushed down my neck, and ate me alive.

Tina screamed bloody murder, pawing at her face and neck.

We thrashed for the doghouse door. Sinking over our heads. Yanking each other, all wheeze and slobber, out onto the ladder. The second I tumbled down, I kicked my sneakers away, ripped off my t-shirt, jeans, my underwear. Fingers raking the hellish, itchy duff clinging to my skin. Unaware of creation till a flashlight clicked on.

Tina, perfectly naked, arms flailing like a person on fire, kept flogging her legs and back with her jeans. Then, shameless as Godiva, in all of her buck-naked glory, she walked over to the policeman, thumbed off his flashlight, and said, "Creep."

"You're trespassing, Tina."

Greg Morton? Three years before, Greg played an all-state first base for Upland High. Now he was a cop? At least he kept the flashlight off till Tina and I shook the evil off our clothes and pulled them back on.

Tina stepped over to Greg and said, "Tell you what. You ride the rooster, and we call it even."

"How do I owe you?" Greg wanted to know.

"You saw me nekked, that's how."

"Doesn't mean I owe you. Or make me a creep."

"Makes you a chicken if you let me down," she said, a salsa troupe of freckles dancing on her face. For as long as I could remember, which feels like forever when you're seventeen, riding the rooster was a legendary prank to Upland misfits because so few of us ever pulled it off. Greg Morton wasn't a misfit, but he was an Uplander, born and raised.

High above, the rooster turned majestically in the harsh floodlight.

"You did your job and chased us off," said Tina. "Then climbed up to check the bird for damages. That's how this goes . . . occifer."

"How'm I s'posed to get up there with all this shit on?" said Greg, freighted with a nightstick, handcuffs, giant ring of keys, radio, gun, silly hat.

"Do it, Greg," Tina said, in that voice of hers.

He flashed an expression more easily imagined than described.

"You think he'll really ride it?" I asked, as we scaled the fence out front.

Tina stared way up at the sky, where the first baseman, in a corona of white light, had returned to all-state form. Standing straight up on the rooster, cool as a surfer at the Banzai Pipeline. Once, twice, three times around for what had to be the greatest rooster ride of them all.

Tina dug the red lipstick from her jeans' pocket, daubed her lips, and planted a big kiss onto the windshield of Greg's squad car.

"Greg Morton is my hero," she said. Three years later, she and Greg got married and moved to Saltburn-by-the-Sea, North Yorkshire, his mother's hometown.

If aliens had come to Earth and asked why they should spare humanity, I would have introduced them to Tina Fernandez, the living daylights, who loved, felt, and let life take her by the hand and live through her. And all our wonky adventures, like facets of my soul, that we shared growing up on Euclid Avenue.

THE THIRD MAN

By the time I staggered back down to the Bottleneck, the sky had grayed over and gusts were blowing me sideways. Dozens had died right here, pinned down by storms while descending from the summit. Like I was. I had to get lower down the mountain to have a chance. I hadn't stopped in nineteen hours and my legs kept buckling every few steps.

I post-holed down through the Bottleneck and traversed left below a headwall of ice, which formed a windbreak—and I saw the natty old North Face tent, tucked into an alcove of black rock, set on an icy pedestal they'd dug out decades before. Warming temperatures had melted the snow that for years had buried the tent, which we'd spotted on the way up, but gave a wide berth because the late, great British alpinist Allan Bancroft was still inside it—and had been for twenty-seven years.

The tent flap was thrown open and I saw, or thought I saw, a hooded figure, waving a gloved hand and yelling, "Come on. Get over here!"

I was worse off than I thought. Seeing and hearing things.

"Don't get in here soon, you're finished . . ."

That got my boots moving. I was too far gone to question the figure, waving from Bancroft's old tent. I kneeled at the entrance.

"Get in and zip the bleeding flap, will you?"

I slithered through the small entrance and closed the flap behind me. That barely left enough room inside to sit upright with my legs outstretched, snugged up against the stranger who was lying flat in a sleeping bag, rimed in hoarfrost and cinched up around his chin. My eyes were so bleary I couldn't focus on anything.

"Drink. You gotta drink."

I still had a thirty-two-ounce hydration bladder of water strapped to my side, under my parka and close to my skin, which wasn't frozen. After all that time above the death zone (26,000 feet), I felt dry as a rock. But the first sip caught in my throat because I was still sucking air. I got a couple swallows down, and my convulsive shivers eased off.

"Where's your partners?"

It took many reedy gasps to say how Selma and Dan, my partners for the summit push, faded at the Bottleneck, around three that afternoon, and descended back to Camp 4.

"And you pushed on?"

I felt okay at the Bottleneck and was hell-bent on bagging K2, the second-highest mountain on Earth. I was only thinking this in fragments—that if I had to solo up and down the 1,000-foot ramp to top out, I would. And did. That made our expedition successful.

"Not till you get down," he said. "And you never do if this tent isn't here. You did a daft thing. And I should know."

I coughed out a few words.

"—Keep drinking. You don't rehydrate, you die right here. Have any gel packs?"

I did. A dozen little packets of energy gel, stuffed into pockets.

"Keep that water coming or you'll gag on that shit," said the stranger.

I got several packs down, with little sips from the bladder. My head started clearing but my eyes kept closing. Then a cold hand smacked the back of my neck.

"Wake up!"

I snapped back. It was dark now. Wind lashed the tent. I could see my breath, but little more.

"No sleeping till you finish that bladder."

I was god-awful thirsty but my throat felt raw and every sip burned going down. Then a poke to my ribs.

"Finish the gel."

That went down a little easier. I managed another two packets. "Keep drinking! You're getting off this thing, mate. Don't forget Joshua Tree. And Christmas in Zermatt."

Joshua Tree was my happy place. And no way could I forget Zermatt for Christmas. Rhonda already bought the tickets. No idea how he knew that.

"Keep drinking," he said. "You got *plans*."

This back-and-forth kept on, with occasional ministrations from the stranger, till I'd almost killed the bladder. I don't remember passing out, only waking up at first light. I unzipped the fly and stuck my head out. A cloud draped the upper massif. Light snow fell, but otherwise dead calm. Selma and Dan's tracks were still visible, next to fixed ropes snaking down into the mist.

I sucked down my last two gel packs with a few sips of water. Several inches of rime had settled over the stranger, still lying flat in his sleeping bag and not moving. I pressed a gloved hand against the bag, wanting to give thanks, but the body inside was frozen solid. I wormed over and looked down at the figure, the sleeping bag cinched around his face—Allan Bancroft's face, white as marble, lips shrunken back in a yellow-toothed rictus, his glossy eyes wide open, staring at forever.

I bolted down to the tents at Camp 4, at 25,000 feet. Selma and Dan were waiting with soup and hot tea. Both were alert but spent. We needed to get off the mountain before the next storm hit. I passed out for an hour, then the three of us tromped down to Camp 2 and we bivouacked there. We made it back to Base Camp late the next day.

We had a big mess tent and the cook made pizza and we celebrated. All the others—especially our Pakistani liaison officer, Colonel Kahn—were dying to know how I'd survived the night out in the open, at 27,000 feet in a storm.

"With difficulty," is all I said. I never climbed again.

A decade later, work took me to London and I bought a big marzipan pineapple and planned to drop it off to Bancroft's widow, having no idea what I'd say. But I learned she'd remarried and moved to Austria, so I ate the pineapple myself—and kept the water coming to get it all down.

WOEFULLY SHORT

Mr. Patrick Maloney checked in with the receptionist, who swiped his insurance card and said the doctor was running a little late. "So kindly take a seat, and keep your mask on at all times."

Maloney sat in a lopsided chair, and would gladly have announced his arrival with a nod or a smile to the others scattered around the waiting room. But all eyes were glued to their phones. Except the young woman sitting directly across from him, wearing trendy transitional glasses with the lenses that darken in the light, so he couldn't see her eyes all that well. Only enough to note that they never acknowledged his existence when he sat down, not eight feet away from her.

Maloney took the high road and absolved the young woman, who evidently didn't know much of anything. Who thought combat boots, with the laces untied, complement a dress? If she called that a dress. Open halter, back-slit something or other. And mint green? He flinched to imagine her, turned out in that ensemble, showing up at his firm for a job interview.

She looked right at him now, with burrowing intensity, which only broke when, with a start, she appeared to catch herself daydreaming. Or more likely, zoning out. This young woman looked hungover if ever Maloney had seen someone, bleary and bewildered after a bender. She'd learn, he hoped. Or she'd end up in a trailer in Pacoima.

A nurse came in for a Mr. Ovitz. When the young woman glanced that way, Maloney saw the orderly cluster of small black dots tattooed on the young woman's shoulder. Was that kind of thing fashionable these days? Maloney chuckled to himself. He didn't know trendy from Yankee Doodle.

After his own daughter—around the young woman's age—got a tribal sleeve tattoo, maybe to spite her Irish ancestors, they barely talked for a month. Now she only called on Christmas, speaking briefly to his wife. He sometimes wondered how his daughter had plunged so far off the rails.

He watched the young woman cast her eyes about the room. As though she owned the place. Judging. He recognized that look. Judging everything she saw with disdain, as though all within eyeshot, possibly starting with him, came up woefully short. A fist clenched in his stomach.

She looked right at him now, the hungover stray from the trailer park. When Maloney held her gaze, she coolly kept taking his measure. He could feel her icy judgement. The fist tightened.

An older woman bustled into the waiting room with two hot drinks, sat in the chair next to the young woman, and handed her a cup, riffing off phrases in Spanish. Which surprised Maloney because neither one looked Mexican.

A nurse came in from reception and said, "*¿Señorita Pérez?*"

"*Aquí mismo,*" the young woman said nervously, getting to her feet.

The nurse came over and offered her arm. The young woman

felt around, pawing air, till she found the nurse's hand, and the nurse led her back through the door.

I REGRET

I regret eating a rotisserie corn dog from 7-Eleven in the summer of 2017.

I regret not getting six guys from the New York Jets to be pallbearers at Mort's funeral so they could let him down one last time.

I regret mixing Prosecco Rosé with the devil's lettuce before Judy's confirmation.

I regret suggesting to Franz a construction-themed wedding, and serving guests Pabst Blue Ribbon beer and Shit on a Shingle (he sure did).

I regret not telling Adriana Flores that I missed her.

ANCIENT HEART

At the beginning of the world, there were giants. And I was there.

The giants were Ancestors-Without-Parents, created from Earthmaker's dance on the margin of void and form.

Before the Ancestors, a dark ocean washed over the shores of nothingness and kissed the edge of night. No music, no remembering, no space between. The Earth just a barren dream in the ancient heart of Earthmaker. Beneath the dream lay stars and sky, sun and moon, the boundless forms of life and experience, all sleeping.

Then a humming, a bottomless energy, throbbing through the emptiness. The humming grew into a Song with such conviction that time split apart: sleeping time and waking time. This moment is called The Dreamtime, when void exploded into life. And I wrote the Song.

The sun burst from the Earth and shone on the empty plain. Earthmaker saw the land was dry and lonely so She cried, and the hollows filled with tears. Under each new waterhole lay an Ancestor-Without-Parent who had slumbered through the eons.

The Ancestors stood up tall as mountains, shaking off the mud. The sun filled their bodies with light. Earthmaker blew life into their lungs and they began walking, singing all things into being: big sand, big forest, big mountains, and creatures who could see. As they sang, the billabong overflowed, the many things rioted over the land, and the offspring sang back: I am snake, I am dingo, I am human. And I heard them singing.

The Ancestors soon tired, ready to return into the Earth to sleep again. Earthmaker took them to the Red Center of the great sand. Of all the living things, only man could lose his way. Earthmaker could not help this, but She could show the Ancestors how to sing the Song into the rock, so humans could find their way back home. And so the Song came to live in Uluru, Ayers Rock, the center of the universe. Many still go Walkabout, retracing the steps of the Ancestors, singing the Song that tells the saga of life.

I have sung with multitudes, to souls so tired they could not speak, to terror so great it rattles teeth. I have sung miracles in high places, in deserts, meadows, and rivers. I have sung with Old Man Sun, who bleaches the bones of the righteous. I have sung quiet moments, friendships shaped by epics, tenderness and understanding offered by strangers who hear the Song truly. I have sung to those forgotten, beaten, scorned, and shamed, the vain and raging and the hopelessly heartbroken, all made whole through the Song.

So now we go Walkabout. I will sing a little of what I have seen of the many I have known, just as the offspring sang back to the Ancestors on the first Walkabout. Only the ancient heart might sustain us, as the Song, written in tears, echoes across the great sand. We all should have a Song to sing when Earthmaker gathers us up and dissolves back into the void, where the dark ocean kisses the edge of night.

—*Adapted from Aboriginal Creation Myths*

INRI

EDGE OF THE CLIFF

Mr. Feyrer led me into the small den and motioned toward a chair.

"Can I get you a sandwich or something?"

"Just ate at my folks', but thanks," I said, as we both continued standing. "Gotta get back to the dorms and start reading all those chapters that I didn't this weekend."

Rita and her mother started quarreling upstairs. Mr. Feyrer tensed up and tried talking over them.

"So, how do you know Rita?"

"We both work on *The Journal.*"

"Rita told us about that," he said, and smiled, but didn't mean it. "Are you two . . ."

"Just classmates."

Mr. Feyrer sagged into the chair he'd offered me. Just above him on the bookcase, between old cloth-bound volumes of *Popular Mechanics* and *Reader's Digest,* stood a small carved effigy of Jesus, hanging on the cross, tiny nails driven through his hands and ankles. Mr. Feyrer didn't look much better.

"She'd rather catch a ride with you," he said, looking at his shoes, "than have her mother and I drive her."

"You're right on my way, so no bother."

The arguing, upstairs, trailed off.

"Rita's changed," he said. "We hardly recognize her anymore."

"I've only known her since the beginning of last semester—"

"But you work with her. You're around her."

True. And we bickered nonstop. Ate Fat Burgers with Fireball chasers. Edited clumsy stories, mostly our own. Confessed secrets and laughed with lumps in our throats.

"You care for someone, you don't let them march off a cliff." He paused, like a man peering into an open casket. "We tried to raise her right," he said, and slumped back in the chair, as though Rita Ann Delmonico was somebody's fault.

"Maybe we can't explain Rita," I said. "But she's gifted. That much I do know."

"That's what they've always told us," he said, staring past me, to a place where none of this happens.

Rita strode into the den and said, "Let's go." Her mother hovered right behind her, fumbling to tuck a packet of Reese's Peanut Butter Cups into the top flap of Rita's day pack.

"Stop, Mom. You're gonna give me diabetes already."

"Comfort food," said Mom. "For when you need it."

Rita tucked the packet of Reese's into her pack and planted a little peck on her dad, whose arms hung limp at his sides.

I had a thought, judging by the size of the Feyrer's small home, as we wheeled onto the westbound 10.

"You an only child?"

"Yeah," she said.

"Well, shit," I said, and immediately regretted it. That house full of grandkids wasn't going to happen for the Feyrers. And all that prickly explaining to friends and relatives. Their flaccid smiles, relieved it was the Feyrer's daughter, not theirs. Things are easier now. A lot. But this was thirty years ago, when they weren't.

"They're not bad people," she said, but the last word died in her throat.

"Your mom futzing over you like that," I said. "They'll never just up and disown you, Rita. No way."

But I didn't know that. We'd both seen that happen more than once.

We drove on in light traffic, riding the edge of a cliff, as the things I admired about Rita, and the things that annoyed me like crazy, blew off her in shards, like a stained-glass window dropped from heaven.

ALIENS STOLE MY DOG

Was moping around the high desert, shattered that Rover had gone missing, when I stumbled across the alien. Even up close, she looked almost human. Dark skin smooth as koa wood. Deep-set hazel eyes. And young. She had a few questions and would gladly hear my answers, if I pleased.

"Ask away," I grumbled. I had some questions as well, but felt too torn up to bother with them.

She showed me her little tablet, thin as a playing card, with a graphic entitled "James Brown's New Year Resolutions," featuring the Godfather of Soul standing next to a short laundry list.

"I understand the words," she said, in a reedy timbre, "but maybe you can tell me what they mean."

I must have scowled. Still thinking about Rover. Licking my face off. Chewing on my cap. How could he up and run off like that?

"Why you so cranky?" she said, touching my arm, her dark eyes warm and true.

"Leave it alone," I said, pushing her hand away. I scanned the first entry on the list: Get offa that thang. "That means stop doing the shit that gets you in trouble," I said. "Like you talking to me." She flushed a little. "You're not supposed to be down here, are you."

Eventually some elder would find her missing, she said, and they'd lock onto her location and reel her back. But she was always so curious about the baffling things we humans did: abstract art, Navajo dances, scat singing. "The whole galaxy has no idea how you people dream up such stuff."

She looked annoyed that I couldn't explain, as her clock kept ticking.

"Make it funky," she said, skipping down her list. "What is this . . . funky."

I peeled the Yankee cap off my head, put it on hers, and said, "You put the cap on your head like so, tilt it to a rakish angle—and you got your funky right there."

She glanced at her tablet, mirroring her image.

"Funky's what you're feeling right now," I said, watching her beam at the cut of her own jib. Made me sore. And suspicious. "What about you guys abducting people," I said. "The anal probes. Leeching off our precious bodily fluids."

"Maybe the Zephrons do that creepy stuff," she said, looking right at me with those honest eyes. "But never us. We only come for two things: dogs—"

"Dogs?" I said, and felt my shoulders rise.

"Transplant some dogs onto a troubled planet and wonderful things happen. I've seen chihuahuas save entire cultures."

"What else you burgle from us?"

"Sitcoms," she laughed.

"So you barge in here, laugh at our jokes, pilfer our pets—"

"Not pets," she said. "Strays. Dogs nobody wants."

But she could only say this while looking away, because she was lying. She'd found Rover alright, wandering around the prickly pears, and she poached him. For herself. Then she snuck back down for more.

She gulped, and her body went stiff. The mothership had locked onto her. I shielded my eyes from the beam as her body flickered, becoming nothing. I lunged for her head, but only got a handful of desert air. Gone. Hot winds riffled the yucca flowers.

Damn. I loved that cap. And Rover.

NEVER HAD TO ASK

a drabble

The kid from Wisconsin strode up to her table in the Windjammers Yacht Club, plunked down a book in front of her to sign, and asked how he might get started with offshore solo sailing. Go to a little lake and practice sailing safely and quickly, she said. Move on to bigger water carefully. The kid looked insulted. What kind of bullshit was this? She never fiddled around on no lake. She just jumped on board a Sadler 24 and pointed the bow toward Mexico. That's true, she said, but I never had to ask anyone how to do it.

BLACK OP

An older Mercedes coupe and new minivan sat on the driveway behind the fence and in front of the two-story, Spanish-style hacienda. A cluster of balloons were lashed to the steel door next to the electric gate for the driveway. The birthday party had kicked off, judging by the music and squeals ringing from the big yard and pool behind the house.

He pulled over by the balloons and walked back to the driveway gate, topped with burglar wire, and looked through the bars at a man cleaning out the minivan with a shop vac. Floor mats, a kid's bicycle with training wheels, beach and sport stuff were strewn over the short tile drive.

"Buenos," he said, clutching a piece of paper with an address. He yelled a second time and a middle-aged man thrust his head from the van and smiled, came over, and opened the steel door, pushing aside the balloons. The man, listed as Ruben Leon on his encrypted brief, had an olive complexion and clever brown eyes.

Ruben Leon hardly looked surprised that the man at the gate, his face painted up like a clown, wore cotton sweats and sneakers. Who'd want to drive in this heat wearing the red shag wig and the whole get-up? And no worries that the clown showed up a little late. Only soccer matches started on time in Argentina.

"You give me a hand with my stuff, I can make it in one trip," said the clown.

"Boriqua?" asked Ruben, using the slang word for Puerto Rican.

"Good ear," said the clown, pausing at the side doors of an old utility vehicle, with no windows in the back. The clown, using an old image of Ronald McDonald he got off the internet, managed his eyes and nose okay, but he'd flubbed the greasepaint around his mouth, so he looked like the saddest man on Earth.

"I've done some work in Puerto Rico," said Ruben. "I'm American, actually."

"Same here, dude," said the clown, switching to English.

Those three words, said like a surfer from Santa Monica, gave Ruben enough pause for the clown to slide open the side door. A second man, crouching inside, reached out with both hands and grabbed Ruben's upper arms. The clown lifted and pushed from behind and Ruben Leon was jerked inside and shoved down, his back flushed up to the panel.

The door slammed shut as the second man dropped into the driver's seat. The clown, squinting from sweat and greasepaint dripping into his eyes, shoved a Mossberg "shorty" shotgun against Ruben's stomach and said, "I wouldn't move."

The van pulled away.

MOUNTAINS, CAVERNS, AND LABYRINTHS

a drabble

Last light bleeds over the western horizon. Too tired to eat much, I make do with nuts and dried fruit, and the quart of water, drawn from Fern Spring, that I'll nurse through the night. The wall below plunges into darkness as shadows chase down the light. I stare at the moon and fall into the far reaches of myself—mansions, caverns, and labyrinths I have wandered for a thousand lifetimes. My name and history mean nothing here. I never see nor hear the sleep that spirits me far away. Light may boast of blinding speed, but shadows always catch me the end.

JUANITO BALA

Paz lagged on the busy sidewalk and watched the Colonel peruse the menu in the outdoor café, occasionally glancing up to squabble with his wife and daughter. The waiter took their orders and Paz walked over and sat down at their table. To her right sat the Colonel's wife, with the tinctured coif and wilting face of an aging beauty queen. She acted put-upon by the unsolicited arrival of the younger Paz, with her chic auburn bob. Paz clasped something in her handbag as she considered the Colonel, sitting directly across from her.

"I believe you have the advantage," the Colonel finally said, looking curiously at the fashionable stranger.

"I do," said Paz, "just as you had the advantage, what . . . has it been a dozen years already?"

"You're confusing me with someone else, I'm afraid. I'm sure we've never met."

The daughter's little smirk said she suspected otherwise.

"I'll never forget your face," said Paz. "And those white spots on your body."

Random flecks of vitiligo, splashed across his hands and neck, contrasted sharply with the Colonel's dark complexion. The wife stared at Paz. The daughter looked at her mother.

"You need to leave now," said the Colonel, his palms pressing into the table.

Paz's brows rose as she rapped the underside of the table. "That's a Browning 9 mil. Take a peek if you'd like."

"What's this 'Browning,' Augusto?" asked the wife.

"Stay calm," said the Colonel.

The waiter set a bowl of raspberry gelato in front of the daughter, a banana split before the wife, and a big *café con leche* for the Colonel. Paz was dying for something, and had been for years, but it wasn't ice cream. The waiter bustled off.

"Who are you?" asked the wife.

"Friends call me Calor. But when I lived here, during *La Resistencia*, they called me Juanito Bala. Aside from a couple gringo instructors at the air base in Honduras, and a few scouts from my rebel group, you're the first people to know that."

"I was here during the war," said the wife. "I know who Juanito Bala was. You're crazy."

The Colonel sat still as a sculpture.

Juanito Bala—Johnny Bullet, in English—was a gangster from an old comic strip. The Sandinistas gave the name to the Contra sniper who kept killing their officers. Over sixty by unofficial count. Right up to the armistice, Juanito Bala had a million-dollar bounty on his head. The Sandinistas never suspected, nor ever discovered, that Bala was a teenaged, former society girl named Paz de la Fé, small-bore rifle champion of Latin America.

"She's crazy, Augusto," the wife repeated. "We're going right now."

"Get up and I'll have to shoot you," said Paz.

"Do as she says," said the Colonel.

The wife looked at Paz and saw the edge of creation, and the big drop below. She froze in her chair, but the gelato was starting to melt.

"Juanito Bala," said the Colonel. "What can I do for you?"

"How old is your daughter?"

"Sixteen," said the mother, "and leave her out of this."

"Sixteen is just a child," said Paz, meeting the girl's eyes. "The world is a *pastille*, and it's all yours. That's how it felt to me. What's your name?"

"Lillibet."

"I was a year older than you, Lillibet, and we'd just returned from a shooting comp in Uruguay. That's when the national coach raped me. So I shot him. And I kept shooting, kept taking from people. But I never got back what I lost." She looked at the Colonel. "You were Lieutenant Zavala back then. In charge of the Army lock-up at Rocas Negras."

"How does she know that?" the wife cut in, cocking her head at the Colonel.

"Because that's where they took me," said Paz. "The national coach was a soldier once, so the authorities would hear nothing about a rape. So off to Rocas Negras."

Paz tapped the underside of the table again and looked at the Colonel.

"The Browning's trained on Lillibet. Tell us what you did to me in that jail of yours, and your daughter lives. Lie . . ."

"The Contras sacked the stockade and dragged you off," he blurted. "That's all that ever happened."

Paz frowned at Lillibet, who turned to her mother, her lower lip quivering.

"How about your wife?" said Paz. "Will you give her up as well, just to keep your secret?"

The muscles flexed in the Colonel's jaw.

"Say something, Augusto," said the wife.

"There is no secret!" he said. "You've got it all wrong here!"

Paz brought up her hand, warning the Colonel to check his outbursts. Several others had already glanced over.

"You'd sacrifice your own family to protect that pride of yours," said Paz, almost whispering. "As you wish. But you'll have to die to keep it this time." She reached under the table with her free hand and chambered a round in the 9 mil. "Or you can tell us the truth, my Colonel, and maybe you'll live. The Browning's aimed right at your belly."

"You deserved it," he said, sneering.

"Would Lillibet deserve it?"

"Lillibet didn't shoot a man in cold blood."

"Lillibet didn't get raped. Once, twice—a hundred times."

"What is she talking about?" said the wife, yanking at the Colonel's sleeve.

"For most of a month, the Colonel here let his men into my cell," said Paz, as a matter of fact. "Then, after the others had their way with me, he'd come in and do it himself. Always last."

They all braced for a gunshot. Paz let them squirm.

"You've got a few more of those white marks, don't you, Colonel. Down below."

The wife made a terrible sound and dumped the Colonel's *coffee con leche* over on the table. She glanced at Paz, who thrust her chin toward the road. The wife grabbed Lillibet and stormed off. The Colonel shifted so the coffee didn't drain onto his pants. Paz brought up the pistol, holding it flat against the tabletop, and pointed right at him.

"If you came here to kill me, I'd be dead already," said the Colonel. "So what do you want?"

Her eyes never left the Colonel.

"I came hoping for answers," she said, then shook her head.

"What happened at Rocas Negras . . . You were just doing what you've always done. I happened to be there, trapped in a cage. It was all as meaningless as our wars. Or killing you now."

She slowly got up, and the Colonel said, "It was wrong. What I did."

"I'm not shooting you, Colonel."

"You just killed my family," said the Colonel, raising his hands.

"It's your turn now," she said, leaning into the words. "Maybe you blow your brains out. I've been there myself. A hundred times. Maybe the wife does you the favor. I give you a year, either way."

The gelato was so much purple soup in the bowl.

Paz tucked the pistol into her handbag, walked out onto the street, and Juanito Bala melted into the passing crowd.

PLAIN AS DAY

We were 184 days on the Appalachian trail. Moby Dick—the great white pack on Tina's back—was so empty it finally weighed less than she did. I wrenched my ankle on the muddy scramble to the top of Mount Katahdin, which marks the end of the 2,190-mile trek. I set my phone on timer for a "summit photo," an obligatory ritual for thru-hikers. Whether we smiled from joy or relief is an excellent question, but an action shot could never show us this frank—filthy and tattered, skinny as rails, arms wrapping the other, holding each other up. Both of us grinning directly at the camara. Later that year, we got married. Then jobs, decent money, catfights, barbecues, miscarriages, mortgages, twin girls, ski trips, booze, flings, separations, bankruptcy, reconciliation, windfalls, awards and commendations, graduations, funerals, and those desolate times, stuck in traffic, wondering how come and what if, moments when we struggle to remember our lives. But whenever we dig out the old summit photo, we know one thing immediately and for sure: That's us, plain as day.

BRIDGE OF SIGHS

She stared at me with the resolve of a bullet. I stared right back and her eyes popped and shot off, as if someone behind her just screamed. She had to be crazy, the way she fitfully wrung her hands and shifted foot to foot, aquiver in her thrift store sneakers, sweatpants, and faded Pokémon t-shirt.

I needed caffeine, so I moved toward the entrance as others hurried out, blocking my view of the crazy girl. But I carried her face in my mind: her sloe-blue eyes, her buzzcut hair you might find on a convict. I put her around twenty-five. Who named her? Where did she go on Thanksgiving?

There she was again, hovering a ways back from the door, her eyes still locked on me, like I owed her my attention. I stepped toward her.

"I hardly slept last night and I'm busy as hell, so quit staring and making me squirm. Here's a couple bucks. Don't care how you spend it so long as it buys my escape and you become nothing again."

That's what I thought but didn't say because I didn't sense she wanted money, which was all I had to give.

I studied the rune of her face but couldn't read it. So I pushed past the pesky panhandler guarding the front entrance, walked to the counter, and ordered a coffee, clueless that COVID-19 lurked behind the espresso machine and soon we'd get dump-trucked into our homes, no exit. How quickly we'd close the distance on the crazy girl.

I got my joe, walked back outside and straight into the girl, who reeled back and vibrated in place. After a few false starts she said, "Can you help me? I need something to drink." Up close, she looked surprisingly clean, and smelled like lavender soap.

"What would you like?"

"Maybe . . . a coffee."

"Take this one," and I handed her the cup. "I added a little milk, to take the curse off it."

She leveled her eyes on me, fighting to hold her ground as some internal vortex kept spinning her gaze away, wrenching her clear of her right mind and through the circus mirror. The sharpest pain was in the repetition and the torment it caused her. Like one of Dante's Lost Souls, cannibalized by beasts and then reconstructed to be eaten again. How could she glitch and shudder and still talk with no hitch in her words or phrasing? And why did she keep staring like she knew me? Who abandoned this girl to pester busy people like myself? I'd dropped off a watch to have the battery replaced, so time meant little till I returned to Swiss Wrist and got busy again.

"How 'bout we sit for a second," I said, motioning towards several empty tables on the sidewalk. "I got some time. A little, anyhow."

She didn't move, holding the coffee close to her chest. I sat and held her gaze as calmly as I could. I told her my name and watched her slowly sidle toward a chair. Finally she sat, her eyes briefly locking on me before jerking away, back on me and off again. Her bony frame jumped each time, like someone ripping Band-Aids off their face.

"So, what's your name? From around here?"

She didn't say a word. I talked about myself, rounding off the edges and fashioning a person who never existed in the way I described him. Not a peep. The disturbing fist-clenching and slow-writhing only eased when I stopped talking and trying to do something. A truck backfired on the road and we both jumped.

"That scared me," she said.

"Scared me too," I said.

She looked at me again, a private gaze she held for a beat before her eyes tore away once more. Little tics still shot through her, but that flash of clear sky in her eyes was enough to light the sonder. Somehow, the person sitting across the table experienced her life with the same boggling range that I did. That we all did. This girl was so thrown-open that the whole thing physically moved her, which, through contagious example, lowered my drawbridge and it all came rushing at me. The kid with a plastic sword running like a ram along the sidewalk, chased by the *Salvadoreño* with the leaf blower. And the older lady who stole a parking space, pissing off the bottle-blonde behind her who jumped from her Jeep and slammed the door, unaware of having the luxury to choose her problems.

I'd lost the need to talk. Her dark energies stopped arcing so hard. Only the random shudder. When her hand took the cup from mine, I saw little remnants of glittery blue polish on several nails. At some other time and place, prettification mattered. Was she ever on someone's guest list? Were there Amber Alerts for crazy people? And what did crazy actually mean?

As we passed the venti coffee cup back and forth, I found myself floating. Like being inside a tear, light sparks darting from the surface. The stillness startled me. I didn't want to leave.

The young woman, casually sipping the coffee, no longer twitched or stared at me, as I no longer stared at myself. We sat there, linked by a bridge of sighs. How long had she imagined this song without words, only heard when shared? How had she known to share it with me? Such a lark, this random stray in her thrift store clothes. For a moment, fraying at the edges, she might have been the ideal human being.

We finished the coffee and I had to get my watch. She walked with me to Swiss Wrist, a few blocks away. Step by step, the distance stretched between us and the demons took her back. I left her on the sidewalk, hands clenching, eyes wrenching to and fro, and went in to get my watch. When I came back out, she was gone.

JUGGERNAUT

Early this morning, we passed the final logging camp and forged into primary terrain. The forest reared higher, the river narrowed, the current quickened, the old barge slowed.

We hugged the bank against the current and plied through curtains of green light slanting from the trees. Locals call it *el salón verde*, the green room. Gnarled ropes looped down, dangling in midair, flecked with black orchids and strangler figs. Bullfrogs croaked from fetid streams emptying into the river. Twice we passed mangrove coves bellowing the mad chorus of howler monkeys.

Every few hours, we'd chug past a small settlement marked by the meager homes of the caboclos, the mixed-race people of the lower Arce. Their thatched hovels, set high on wooden piles, overlooked the river from above the monsoon line. Now and again, the captain would veer around islets of rushes in the river shallows, his hands slow-dancing with the giant ship's wheel. I milled around the stern, smoking Brazilian cigarettes and staring into the trees.

The engine clanked like hell. The pilot, fighting the current, pulled over at a small abandoned settlement half a mile upstream, and tied off to a cannonball tree at the waterline. Several decaying, oblong huts stood in the small clearing. The pilot and the boy worked below while we panted in the bow, soon forced off the boat when most of a grimy diesel engine covered the open deck.

The pilot mumbled a few sentences, motioned toward the huts, handed me a sledgehammer, and went back below. Portuguese was close enough to Spanish that I usually caught the gist.

"He says the sun's going fast and they need a fire to work by," I told Dwight. "He's got to make Raul by Thursday and can't waste a day on repairs. We can strip the wood off those huts to build the fire."

"What about the people?" Dwight asked.

I glanced toward the huts. "The pilot said they all died last year. Measles."

We climbed a notched log and stepped into the first hut, sobered by the wooden basin, the carved stool, the manioc grater, as if carelessly left there yesterday.

We went back outside and laid into the hut with the sledgehammer. In an hour, we had a growing pile of bamboo, reeds, and hardwood joisting, and a fire licking thirty feet into the air. The sky was dark and starless. All night, the pilot and the boy tinkered with the engine, and all night, Dwight and I worked the fire to keep the light high enough to slant into the boat, our shadows dancing over the somber screen of trees.

My eyes were occasionally drawn to the prow of the barge, where a brass nautical figurehead—one of Neptune's angels—was welded in place, her features so gouged by river boulders and deep green rust she couldn't possibly see us. But I kept checking to make sure, feeling like a grave robber as we bashed away.

By the wee hours, we burned through the last of the hut, and

Dwight and I took turns sledge-hammering the pylons until they worked loose and we could draw them from the gluey soil and roll them into the fire. The engine fired over and the pilot waved us back aboard.

Behind us, a mound of coals smoked and crackled. In a week, the rising current would claim the cinders and the jungle would creep over the small clearing. Rain and wind would salt the ruin and, in a matter of months, there would be nothing but a solitary pylon to tell a traveler that people had lived and died here.

Rain beat down from one black cloud, the blood-red sun beside it. Steam welled off the moving water—dull, hanging, and so thick I could taste my own hot breath. Thunder clapped through the green corridor, followed by sheets of blistering rain.

Near sunset, the river leveled off, and on both sides, the green hedgerow ran straight ahead, a long, hushed foyer tapering into the night. Far in the highlands, outlined one against the other, the crests of a high cordillera were shuffled like a deck of stony cards—brusque peaks, bluish draws, jutting arêtes swaying, rising, falling in the harsh light, ever more inaccessible as we motored on.

The pilot maneuvered to the middle of the sleeping river, now a hundred feet across, and lowered the anchor. A mile ahead were more cataracts, said the pilot, and the three hours between us and the next settlement were the trickiest yet. He'd need all the daylight to navigate this stretch. We moored for the night.

The whole sky fell all at once. Through the rainy gray pane, the land loomed void and dark. The deck swirled shin-deep. We stripped to shorts and stood in the bow, the hot rain pocking the water. Then only an electric silence, and the feeling of pure duration. The pilot gestured toward the left shore and said, "Urupa."

Two forms came into focus, and we saw these ghostly shapes were alive, squatting on their heels, their faces cast in irrefutable sneers. Somewhere in the bush around them lurked their clansmen, the dusky, bleeding sacrifices of an industrial juggernaut adding nothing to the beauty of their land or the life of their souls. "Wilderness," which had always indicated the original and untrodden, increasingly suggested black magic acts of disappearance. In a few years, the world around us—the trees, the natives, El Salon Verde itself—would silently pass from sight, like a new moon burning on inky water.

HAPPY TRAILS

“How ’bout we take fifty bong rips,” said Rudy, “bomb up to Apple Valley, and visit Roy Rodgers’ Western Museum?”

About ten of us had planned a big mountain bike ride. Then Sunday brought nothing but rain, leaving us nothing to do; so getting our herb on and crashing Roy’s dusty old cowboy museum seized on our boredom and had half of us piling into beater cars and gunning it out the San Bernadino Freeway. Except when we got there, the museum was “Closed on Sundays.” I checked a back door, found it ajar, and we slipped right in.

The museum was dark except for a halo of light around a big diorama. We were drawn there by Roy’s lush baritone, which had to be a recording, and which I recognized from *Rodeo Dough, The Cowboy and the Señorita,* and fifty other Roy Rodgers B-movies and grainy old reruns some of us watched as kids. None of this landed for the younger riders among us, caught in a ganja-and-rawhide time warp.

We hunkered in deep shadow across from the diorama, which housed a saguaro cactus, a tumbleweed, and a pastel sunset sketched on a rear wall. And damned if we weren't looking right in on ol' Roy himself, eighty if a day, turned out in his go-to-meeting duds, with his green silk neckerchief and embroidered chaps. Even wore his nickel-plated shooting irons.

Roy sat a little broadside on his Golden Palomino, Trigger, which was stuffed and who, when it was still hauling mail, won a PATSY Award for its role in *Son of Paleface*. A few feet behind reared Buttermilk, also stuffed, the faithful steed of his beloved wife, Dale Evans (a stroke had borne her away the previous autumn). Just left, caught in mid-air, hung Bullet the Wonder Dog, stuffed as well, and who'd accompanied Roy on many adventures in Mineral City.

Roy had a load on and kept strumming his guitar and pouring all of himself into "Blue Shadows on the Trail." A lonesome tableau: Roy's pick raking across five strings, drawing one truth—that all hearts are broken and we all must die. It all just caught in my throat. But the whole thing was dead wrong. Dead as lost moments, fossilized in a diorama. Wrong as a forgotten old cowboy trying to stuff and strum and sing these hoary relics into a present where they didn't belong.

Then Roy crawls off Trigger, wobbles out of the diorama, and returns with a big Raggedy Ann doll—or something—draped over his shoulder.

Roy gently positions the ragdoll up on Trigger, gets situated back in the saddle, and starts strumming his guitar. But Raggedy Ann keeps flopping forward and her red Stetson tumbles off. That's when we saw the face of this—*thing*—red lipstick smeared around its gob and a Frankenstein gash, stitched with rawhide, jagging down its forehead.

Roy keeps strumming, belting out, "It's Home Sweet Home to Me," and we keep staring, thinking to ourselves, *This can't be*. Ray Ortega finally said it.

"That's Dale Evans, man. He stuffed her."

For minutes, it felt like, we stared in a trance, as the only four lines of cowboy poetry I knew kept repeating in my head:

> *But things have changed now, we are poorly clothed and fed.*
> *Our wagons are all broken and our ponies most all dead.*
> *Soon we will leave this country, you'll hear the angels shout,*
> *"Oh, here they come to Heaven, the camp-fire has gone out."*

We slipped out of the museum as quietly as we'd snuck in, leaving the former Sheriff of Mineral City, with the broken and the dead, strumming his guitar, waiting for the angel's shout.

BOUNDLESS SHADOW OF WILLOWS

My folks were buried side by side, so I could make my living amends in one go.

I drove my parents mad. Mama pined. Dad, whose kid brother went down in a B-29 Superfortress, lashed out hard. All of us living on a fault line of fear.

Sunday morning. In August. Driving out the 60 towards Ontario, California, felt like going to hell. I surfed the acid rock stations.

Narrow streets latticed the cemetery, huge as a green ocean. My sister gave me coordinates so I eventually found Evergreen Lane, but didn't have the row number and spent forty-five minutes crisscrossing nowhere. Maybe because I was in no hurry to find them.

Imagine trying to locate two flat gravestones among tens of thousands peppered across several square miles of Bellevue Memorial Park. Generations of settlers, pushing west, settled in the Greater Pomona Valley, and most of them were buried right here. More looping around.

I finally found my folks, next to a withered bouquet lying aside the grass marker of a person dead forty years. I hadn't returned here since burying my parents—I couldn't remember the dates. I'd brought no flowers. Nothing extra to try and leave behind.

I sat in the grass, my eyes fixed on the "Mama" above my mother's name, chiseled in slate. Her own mom had died when she was eight, and she couldn't bear hearing the word "Mother." So my sister and I called her Mama; that's how it had to be. Much of our lives were hamstrung like that. I cringed to remember the few times a reckless or juiced-up relative mentioned Tommy.

Thomas Allen Mitchell, the stillborn child Mama had two years after I was born. His memory slayed her. Dad insisted we keep Tommy dead and gone. No questions. Never say that name. So Tommy lived, feral and wraithlike, in our imaginations.

I stared at my father's grave, clueless who was buried there. We'd never talked about anything, never asked each other questions, so we never lived out loud. Never gelled into recognizable shapes. We were, all of us, strangers to ourselves and to each other.

My grandmother, Ruth, was my only anchor to the world. She told me things, burgled from my family's secret trunk, chained by the shame and blue funk that haunted our dinner table. Gritted teeth whenever someone went off-script or was swept into the open, because even Dad couldn't stage manage the world. The unstated blew out in Dad's rage, in Mama's fugitive heart. Our two cats hid under tables. But that trunk never blew entirely open—till it did, quite unexpectedly, as I shifted on the grass by their graves.

Why had I always lacked the soul glue that might connect me to others? How could people blend so naturally, with a sense of belonging lost on me, asphyxiated by the emotional charades I learned from my parents, who learned it from their parents, and which drove us all mad. All those family ghosts, doing unholy things. Throttling our lives. The wise paid them enough care and attention to weaken their curse—or so I imagined. I lived at the speed of Snapchant, where nothing still or serious could touch me. In a present so trampled under, I gasped for air—and knew I had to find Tommy. The plan flew out of the ground, thrust topside by my parents, so both Tommy and I might live above ground. Had the plan made sense I would never have bothered.

I'd passed the children's section while driving in, knowing Tommy was buried there. But the office was closed on Sundays. So much for getting directions. I cast off, fording across that green ocean towards the children's section, hundreds of yards and lifetimes away.

My feet moved on their own, till I caught myself tromping over gravestones, which felt like a desecration. I glanced down, marking my steps, and my eyes fell directly on my grandmother Ruth's grave. One among tens of thousands. Bizarre. Grandma had learned to be invisible, to never trust people who dramatized their life. But I promised to stay the course just the same. I was questing for her grandson, after all.

The children's section lay in the shade of gnarled willows, ringed by a lichen-flecked stone wall. Passing through the narrow entrance destroyed all thought, the space was so still and so somber. Several newer headstones mixed with those reaching back a century. I quietly read a few names out loud. Few of those buried here had lived more than a year or two.

A man and a woman, neither older than thirty, slowly walked past, with expressions that had no name in any language.

I found Tommy's grave in minutes. Silently introduced myself and sat down, realizing I was one of a few living people who even knew he'd existed.

Existed? He'd been born dead. An unpackable notion made meaningless as figure slowly emptied into ground. Dry leaves rustled. I could hear, it seemed, for a million years.

Valéry once dreamed of this incandescent space, where nothing distinct exists, where nothing lasts, but where nothing is truly destroyed. In the boundless shadow of willows, the difference between being and not being, between Tommy and I, dissolved into a felt sense of living death. Knowing in my bones that all of us, all apparent things, were written in rain. Shadows and ghosts. Nothing substantial. Nothing to call my own. I turned to stone.

You never find safety in a graveyard. No shelter from these monuments of loss, which zero out the center, uproot every anchor, and burn all reason to ash.

The ground gave way and I plunged. Past all secrets, past the eternal human madness, fear, as my resentments and rebelliousness, my scathing indifference, calved away, till only connection remained. *Sui generis.* Utterly placeless. Yet all that really was. Sometimes sensed in torch songs, on high overlooks. In her sudden laugh. Between the penumbra of a stillborn brother and a prodigal son.

There are shadows where those who left arrive in a tidal drift of filling and emptying. Shadows we pass through and feel but can never hold. Where the soul glue sets only when we yield and cast away. The moment I did, Tommy and I were both finally born.

DUNROBIN CASTLE

a drabble

A regiment of creaky old men, turned out in argyle kilts, basking in the glory days of Crown Rule, smirked at Poppy's sandals, paisley bucket hat, and tie-died tee.

All around her in the Edwardian-style gallery, staring down from the walls, were hundreds of trophy heads—ibex, springbuck, warthog, tiger—each slain during African safaris, by the noblemen who once lived here in Dunrobin Castle.

"I heard you men kill these big animals," said Poppy, smiling at the duffers, "and mount them like this because you believe they are beautiful. Makes me wonder what you do with your wives?"

CHINGADERA

THE REAL CHINGADERA

I first ran into Lance during a fundraiser at The Broad.

"Laura Blackburn," he said, smiling. "The landscape painter." I felt a little something that he knew who I was, and I told him so.

"I could just murder a burger about now," he said.

Ten minutes later, we were at Hamburger Hamlet, where I fell in love with his animal spirit. We hardly left each other's sight for the next three months.

I lived in Chatsworth, over the hill from his place in the Palisades; but after a week, I loaded my van and moved in with Lance at his compound, a converted stable. He had scads of room. Now I could watch him work.

The best stuff dazzles and intrigues, but Lance's work always looked like truth. He'd grok onto a scene or a subject and shuffle around like a douser seeking groundwater. Then paint flew off his brush in loose, rapid strokes that, up close, looked like formless smudges of impasto. Step back and the swipes and smears unified into God's own blueprint.

When he grokked onto me, with his raw basal intensity, we were two souls clinging to an asteroid—and one another, never quite getting hold of either. Strong meth for a wannabe art star like myself, barely thirty (Lance was thirty-two), though in many ways I was older by an age than Lance Rincon, a rascal in a man's body.

An alum of Lance's from the ArtCenter College of Design told me Lance first showed up on full scholarship. "And poor as dirt. They only covered his tuition," she said, "so for that first semester, Lance lived in his VW."

That night, not mining for secrets, I asked Lance what kind of childhood he had.

"Short," is all he said. Half the time I swore he was still in it.

We'd attend at a gala dinner or a gallery opening and if Lance got hungry, he would start eating mousse with his fingers. He went to the Temple Beth synagogue, for a neighbor's bar mitzvah, in jeans and a hoodie. And sometimes he got dark and would isolate or body surf all day instead of talking and dealing. Less is more worked for Lance, but it never worked for me. I couldn't find him in my heart because he couldn't stay there, only visit, only binge, guns blazing. I started feeling depleted.

I once woke to find Lance lying next to me with a sketchpad and a couple charcoal sticks. He kept fussing and erasing and rubbing the colors with his fingers. "I can't nail your skin tone," he said.

"Are you looking at me, or my skin tone?"

He lay back on the bed, like a snow globe recently shaken, the swirling white stuff obscuring the figure inside. All but his eyes, reflecting back the lonely abyss of his soul.

I couldn't blame him for trying the impossible, chasing after something more basic than love. But even his best work could never love him back. Nothing, it seemed, ever could. I kept reaching for this man in his agon with himself, even as he reached for me. We never closed the gap.

One morning, as we silently ate breakfast, he said that he couldn't blend, or even be with people—not for long anyway. But he couldn't help but try to hold onto me till I found that out. That afternoon we loaded my stuff into my van.

I ran into Lance, mostly in passing, over the next four or five years, though he sent me roses every birthday and a gift certificate to Macy's every Christmas. I didn't know if the favors were for services rendered, or because he felt guilty, or what. Then I saw him on a BBC video, and he looked and sounded nothing like the Lance I remembered: a tribe of one. The sweetest boy I never knew. Something had impelled him to grow all the way up, and I had to find out what. Next time I heard Lance was in town, I texted him I was on my way, and don't you dare leave.

"About time you showed up," he chuckled, leading me into his studio. "Now that you're all famous and shit."

Not hardly. I'd only recently gotten enough work into galleries that I no longer had to waitress or work retail. As we walked, a girl, maybe thirteen, strode up and showed Lance a sketch of a seascape, impressively fashioned for someone so young. Lance studied the sketch and said, "I can't do that."

"Liar," she smiled, and rushed off.

"You teaching a little these days?" I asked, intrigued that Lance, so busy and, by then, so wealthy, should ever find time for others.

"Take a look."

He led me into the rear atelier, where a dozen scruffy, defiant students, all in their teens, were drawing, working in charcoal, watercolor, oil. Really getting after it.

We paused by an Asian girl in hand-me-down clothes, painting one of Lance's other students, slouched in a ragged wicker chair and mugging in a silly hat Caesar might have worn to lead his legions into the wonders of an unknown world. The girl had all of

Lance's economic style. A flick here and a daub there and—Voilà. You could read more in the painted face than in the real one. It scorched imagination to think where she might take this.

Lance hailed the others, to admire "The Real Chingadera," as he called the girl's portrait, while Caesar took all the credit. The others gathered round and went off, pelting Caesar with whatever wasn't tied down, then dove back into their own projects, working like their lives depended on it. To save and be saved. Which is the only way you ever create like that.

COACH

WATERMELON SMILE

Saturday night. Daphne's in Albuquerque, so I ring Grub Hub to drop off some Thai food. Squid salad. Massaman curry. Even got the spicy crab noodles. Then settle in for the Lakers game when my internet craps out. Half-read books are piled on chairs and end tables, but I feel like checking out, not in. So I head to High Q dispensary for some herb. Not a regular thing. Call it a treat.

And who do I see there but Coach Haggarty, my football coach from high school. And like, sixty. Back in the day, Coach would bark us through "hell week," the first stretch of summer practice, till we'd drop and start puking. Guy had no chill, but he had a big heart. One time we're fumbling through a tip drill. Coach comes over and says, "Stop. Only thing you're practicing is how to do it wrong." Wrong as finding my old coach at the weed shop. Wrong as me burning a fatty before the board meeting—I don't do it often. Can't have people calling me a stoner. Least of all my Coach, whose assessment I fear, after all these years.

High Q is packed and I take cover behind a girl with a puffy and big hair. But Coach spots me straight off and storms over.

"Archie!" he says, working my hand like a pump handle. "So great to see you. How long's it been?" His voice, forged on the gridiron, carries like thunder. Surprised the glass bongs haven't crashed to the ground, the way he goes on. Everyone's staring.

"Had my knee scoped a few years back," I say, answering a question Coach never asked. "A little . . . product helps with the pain. As needed."

"So I've heard. But for me," says Coach, with a watermelon smile, "I just like gettin' high."

CULTURAL ICON

The empty hearse and the last cars rolled away, leaving us sitting on a cold marble bench.

"The adventures of Dora De Vos were better than Larson and La Carré," he said, handing me his card: *Sam McCaffery. Senior Special Agent. Art Crime Team. Federal Bureau of Investigation.*

Dora had told me about Sam, who, after her last round of chemo, had grilled her—graciously, but six ways to Sunday. He looked younger than I'd imagined.

"Last weekend," said Sam, "I checked out Dora's early works. Over at the Skirball Center. She should have been a cultural icon, Mr. Gaines, not some knockoff artist."

I'd just buried the woman, and wasn't in the mood.

"You never had anything real that ties Dora De—"

"Genkei Soto," he said, slamming in. Sam had some fire in him. So did Soto, a billionaire industrialist under criminal indictment until he got cremated in a car bomb a decade ago. When Japanese authorities patted down Soto's estate, they found Piet Mondrian's *Epistle,* stolen the previous year from the Kunsthaus

Zurich—a theft the world heard all about. Sam, however, kept the case on the hush, and for a dozen years since, the public never learned how the *Epistle* had once turned up at Soto's house. Not until now.

Sam kept eyeing me, with an annoying smirk, waiting for some tell. I lipped a Sherman Slim, but didn't light it.

"Imagine," said Sam, "soon after Soto burns, some curator in Yokohama discovers the word *REPLICA* on the back of the Mondrian. In colorless dye that only appeared under ultraviolet light."

I never liked that touch, but Dora insisted. I lit the Sherman.

"National Intelligence in Japan suspected an American crime ring, fencing fakes," he said, "so they dial up the Agency, who dumped the case on me."

"Talk about flying blind."

"Nothing but. Till I discovered New York art dealer Sid Abrams had hawked a' O'Keeffe and a Hopper to Soto. And bugged off to Tokyo, shortly after the Mondrian got nicked."

Immigrations showed Abrams visiting Russia, Qatar—a string of countries—probably fencing bum *Epistles* ten times over, Sam rambled on. Then six months ago, a decade after the Kunsthaus job, Sid Abrams drops dead.

"He smoked too much," I said. "Word is, Sam, you took early retirement. And closed the case as well."

"Last Tuesday," he said. "Right after I learned of Dora's passing."

Which is why we were sitting there, under the jacarandas. The rest arrived as falling pedals—that the Art Crime Program had little truck with the Soto ruse and played along as a professional courtesy; but Sam McCaffery had spent ages dogging this down, and had to know. So the year before, he took a flyer and videoed guests at Sid Abram's memorial.

"That's how I made Dora De Vos. And you," he said. "Couple

weeks after you shoveled dirt on Abrams, the Mondrian—the real one—is returned to the Kunsthaus in an unmarked DHL crate in mint condition. I connected the dots from there."

"Dora liked you for some reason. Never told me why."

Sam glanced over at the mound of chrysanthemums heaped on Dora's grave and said, "Give me one of those Shermans." I lit two, and gave one to Sam.

"I came back from the Middle East in a hundred pieces," he said. "That first summer, took me months to crawl out of the bottle. The only place I could stand being alive was in art galleries."

"A purist," I said. "Good on you, Sam. But the way you have it, Dora faked the stuff that saved you. So either you've bungled the story—"

"Somebody pinches the Mondrian and throws it to Dora," he said, me wondering how many times he'd run this through his mind. "She's a world-class painter, and also the Head of Restoration at the Huntington—so who better to style the knockoffs than Ms. De Vos? Abrams fences the baloneys to shady tycoons. Nobody's wise to your grift, but they keep your secret, believing they're holding ganked art—till Soto goes down in flames."

He toed the Sherman into the dirt.

"Art was sacred to Dora De Vos. That's why she labeled her fakes and returned the original without a mark. So what if she builds a nest egg off the spare change of sheiks and bandits. All thanks to you."

I went to talk and he said, "Don't even. You two were an article once, but she wouldn't go for marriage, so you fashioned the grift to keep your old squeeze cozy. And with that shipping company of yours, you can move anything, anywhere, unmarked." He smiled this time. "You're a romantic, Mr. Gaines. And you went to Cornel with Sid Abrams."

Which didn't explain why charges were never made.

"Some gangster learns Abrams sold them a phony; he's found toes-down in a week. A man like you would know that. So you wait till Sid's buried to return the Mondrian. No harm, no foul. That's how I played it."

And he never made the agency the wiser. Sam looked smug at making such a call. My turn to smile. I handed him an envelope.

"That's from Dora. The Mondrian hanging in the Kunsthaus is one of Dora's fakes. With the *REPLICA* left off."

Sam stared at the envelope.

"The key inside's to a climate-controlled storage unit in Playa Del Rey. The *Epistle* is in there. The real one."

Sam opened the envelop and peered inside.

"Dora was a purist, like you, Sam. But she couldn't bear to part with the original. Not while she was alive. I think she felt curious what you'd do with a masterpiece in your hands."

Sam took the key from the envelop and held it up, at arm's distance, in the fading light.

"The one thing you never got about Dora De Vos," I said, "was her wicked sense of humor." Sam kept staring at the key laying in hand. "Don't lose that," I said. "There's not a spare."

Only slowly did Sam's fist close around the key.

"Give me another one of those Shermans," he said.

TRINITY ON TRINITY

A new "inspirational" platform called Celeb Bulletin ("Evidence-Based") popped up on my Google homepage. Today's entry reads:

Trinity McClean in Bathing Suit is "Back in the Breakers"

(A high-res color photo shows Trinity—sultry smile, tricolored macrame headband, oversized designer shades—stylishly laying across some black lava rocks, her sweeping globes busting out of a Persian blue bikini she stows in an acorn shell. Creaming combers curl in the background.)

Trinity McClean, star of the Netflix hit *Pansexual Surfer Girls of Hawaii,* is back in Oahu, where they film the show. The twenty-two-yea-old actress—who keeps a luxury condo in Maui—has been open about both her mental health struggles and her triumphs. How does Trinity do it?

Trinity is Vegan

"Last year I went paleo," said Trinity, "and all that swine went straight to my chest. Nothing to flex about, but kudos to cross-fit because I was born in Alaska. So I upped my game to a facium diet, only eating animals with a face. (Though she allowed herself a cheat day once a week, favoring bunt cake and mimosas.) But, like, a few weeks ago at Geoffrey's, I swear a magpie goose was eyeballing me, straight up from the plate, so I switched to vegan, and try and take a spin class Sunday mornings. The secret is small portions."

Trinity is Pansexual

"I was born with an inclusion mindset," Trinity recently said on TikTok. Such liberal style, however, has occasionally thrown shade on Trinity's character. "Some troll on Twitter said, 'for you free-range Pans, it's any port in a storm,'" wrote Trinity, answering her critics. "Then she says I blew the editor of *'N Style Magazin*e to simply get my photo on the cover. That's so untrue. I mean, the editor works remotely out of Minnewaukan, North Dakota. So with this COVID phooey going on and no flights, plus me trying to learn meditation from the Buddhify App, there was nothing simple about it. Go off . . . I guess."

Trinity Has Narcissistic Personality Disorder

"The psychiatrist gave me my personality disorder when I was eighteen. I could sulk and, like, move to New Jersey or something. Or learn how to honor myself," said Trinity, during her recent break from shooting. "My thoughts and feelings are actually part of me. And you. I admire that about myself. The literature says I'm lacking in the apathy department. But ask anybody on set. I get bored sometimes."

Trinity Sometimes Talks About Herself in the Third Person

"Having enormous tits and a chiseled brisket, a hit TV series, and millions of fans can sometimes blow up an extra self image of

Trinity in Trinity's own body," Trinity told *Me Magazine*. "Trinity's discovered that talking about Trinity in the third person gives Trinity a third-eye perspective of Trinity. Like on the dollar bill. It also allows Trinity to cherish Trinity from heavenly new angles, which Trinity has had the honor of enjoying."

Live Authentically, Trinity Advises

"Never let anyone pressure you to say you are something, or you aren't something else," Trinity recently declaimed on her podcast, *Trinity on Trinity*. "Just don't really let anybody interpret how you're feeling, or anything you're saying, so long as you're inspired. It's all about self-discovery. Like, living authentically, so when the curtain falls—and we're all just fossils in the wind—I can die happily in my own arms. Namaste."

E e
X x
A a
C c
T t
L l
Y y
! !

EXACTLY!

Mrs. Latimer taught Survey of British Poetry and so thoroughly embodied the work that she didn't so much teach verse as she tutored existence.

"You have to know the material by heart," said Mrs. Latimer, when Simon asked about her secret to teaching. "But you also have to know your audience, and that takes a good memory." To remember what? "Depends on your audience." She smiled here, leaving students to discover the details on their own.

Simon's last class as an undergrad involved short stints subbing in the local public schools. Miss Bloom only provided a few notes scribbled on a filing card when Simon took over her fist grade class for the final hour. He felt old memories stir to see nineteen wild-eyed kids giving him the once-over. To break the ice, he introduced himself, going to each student in turn, and asking them a question.

"So, Latoya," he said. "How old is your father?"

"Six years?"

"Six years? How is that possible?"

"He became father only when I was born."

Simon glanced at the other kids, whose faces all said, *Well, yeah. Of course he did.*

"Okay, Jimmy," said Simon, moving on. "How do you spell 'rooster?'"

"R-U-S-T-E-R."

"Sorry, Jimmy, that's wrong."

"Maybe it's wrong," said Jimmy. "But you asked me how I spelt it."

Simon didn't know his audience. But after a few more questions, he started to remember the ruckus.

"Mia, go up to that map on the wall and show the class where North America is."

Mia ran up to the map and jabbed a finger on the North American continent.

"Well done," said Simon, who moved to the next student and said, "Okay, Olivia. Who discovered America?"

"Mia did," said Olivia. Simon burst out laughing.

"Exactly!" he said, thrilled to be a kid again.

LA FÉE VERTE

That banging on the door was my neighbor, Gaston, just returned from France with a liter bottle of liquid, pure and green as an emerald.

"It's not," I said.

"*Il est*," he said. "A 1923 vintage."

The old bottle bore a yellowing white label with a coat of arms flanked by lions, up on their hind legs, and the words: ABSINTHE VERTE.

I'd read a few things about this legendary shine, leached from wormwood flowers and other medicinal herbs. Gaston had discovered the bottle inside a viola case while cleaning out his mother's *château* in Fontainebleau.

"*Repose en paix,* Pauline," said Gaston solemnly. He carefully set the bottle on my ottoman table. "Now we drink, to the memory of *ma mère*. I return with zee utensiles."

Gaston trudged off and I recalled, "When Paris Sizzled," Mary McAuliffe's ode to the *Années folles,* the crazy years, when in salons and cabarets all across Paris, *la fée verte* ("the green fairy") was the go-to libation for writers and artists like Hemmingway and Baudelaire, Van Gogh and Munch. Gaston and I joined them via two quaffs of Absinthe Verte, poured into whisky glasses. Sugar cubes were set on slotted spoons, resting on the rims, over which Gaston, with religious unction, poured chilled water from a carafe.

"*Chin chin*!" I said, clicking Gaston's glass. We tossed the green stuff off.

"*Zut alors*!" Gaston coughed out. "Tastes like zee ass."

We sat slack-jawed, staring at a Corona beer ad flashing on my big screen, where beautiful people, lithe, bronzed, with blinding-white teeth, were bumping and grinding to the salsa music. Heaven. And we needed heaven. Gaston set up another two Fairies and we drank those down. And two more.

A lucid drunkenness stole over us. The Yankee game looked ludicrous; but when the beer ad ran again, I found myself dreaming of a tropical paradise. The impossible beauties and rip-corded Lotharios. White sand stretching to a turquoise sea. Gaston fetched more Fairies, and I plunged through a wormwood hole straight into the beer ad. Except it wasn't an ad or a daydream. It was my life.

I was a cross-fit stud in a chartreuse Speedo, dancing the hip-thrusting *bachado* as the salsa roared. The smoking grill, where a smashing Black girl with wiener tongs flipped peeled shrimp and flamboyant chilies. The gigantic cooler full of frosted Coronas. Like Marry Poppins' bag, you could always retrieve another beer. And Teresa, with the freckles and impossible breasts. Like someone shot two rockets through her back. Leading me across the ice plants to a copse of fan palms, where she humored my Speedo and stripped off her bikini—and I came to on my couch, sucking down ragged breaths. Trembling from the inside. Skin slackened with cold sweat. The room pitched. I reeled to the bathroom and ralphed. Then passed back out on the linoleum—and came to back in heaven.

The sun blazed. The ice had melted in the big cooler and the Coronas were lukewarm. Revelers were tiring, but we all danced on since the sand was too hot to stand. Several angels looked annoyed, especially Teresa, who snarled and slinked away. Whitecaps leaped off the blackening sea. A gust blew sand that stuck like fleas to our sweaty skin. We were starting to get sunburned pretty bad. And hungry. But only a shriveled little brät remained on the grill. And the Black beauty chef, hacking from charcoal smoke, looked like she'd yank my eyes out with her wiener tongs if I reached for it. And turn down that fucking music already.

I moved toward the fan palms, seeking shade, where a girl with sad eyes stared north, toward the jagged outline of ramshackle dwellings rising off the shadowed hillside. Dark figures milled in gloomy doorways.

"What is that?" I asked.

"It's where we go if we ever leave this beach," she said. A bolt of lightning drilled the sand.

I trembled inside, curled in a fetal knot on my bathroom floor. I crawled, more dead than alive, back to my den and slithered onto the couch. I felt like the paper plate beneath a sloppy joe. I reached for the carafe of water. Empty. No way I could make it to the kitchen. I closed my eyes, plunged down the wormwood hole, and face-planted onto the beach.

The ocean roiled in the distance. The sun blazed like a trillion blowtorches. Blisters welled off our shoulders, backs, and the tops of our feet. My throat burned but the water boiled in the cooler, where the Coronas exploded like grenades. Then fire swept over the ramshackle structures in the distance. People, burning alive and screaming, ran down the hillside, never reaching the beach. We bunched together, shrieking, as our flesh began to bubble.

Then surrounded by a burning ring of fire. We fell to the sand, and the flames went higher.

My hysterical cries jerked me awake. I knew why Van Gogh cut off his ear. Why Munch painted *The Scream*. Gaston swayed before me, clutching the bottle in shaky hands, green fairies dancing in the jade liqueur. He looked like Waterloo.

"We only drink zee half of it. *Putain de merde!* What will we do?"

I felt like I'd caught dengue fever. Remembered Hemmingway, blowing his brains out with a shotgun. Grouchy old alki forgot the prime directive: When in doubt, ramp it up.

"Better drink the rest," I said.

SHOOTER

No one had entered the suite since her last visit, a conclusion based more on predatory instinct than on the undisturbed articles she had left there the night before. Aside from a little light bleeding in from the bathroom, the main room was dark as night.

Petite hands removed a votive candle from a cellophane baggie, placed it on a saucer, and lit the wick. A red carnation, her macabre calling card, floated in a half-filled glass beside the candle on the table. In the pre-dawn stillness, the bouquet of the bloom hung gently in the little demesne.

The wig and the fat suit, used to hoax the security camaras, were carefully laid out on the floor. With such short hair, a hairnet was merely a precaution. She talced her hands, gingerly pulled on latex gloves, and secured the crepe surgeon's booties with rubber bands and a wrap of athletic tape. Her jogging outfit now covered every bit of exposed skin save her face, peering out dispassionately from her loose hoody. Even if forensics could scrub her DNA off something, no one, least of all anyone here in the States, had genetic markers to run a match.

The previous evening, she had photographed the front room with her iPhone, had studied the images, charted the layout, and devised a simple plan. She again measured the height of the tabletop with the steel tape and correlated with the middle window looking straight out of the suite. She outlined a fifteen-square-inch box on the glass with a grease pencil, and once more acquired and confirmed the measurements.

She took the Dremel tool from a pocket on the side of the golf bag and screwed the mini circular saw attachment into place. She moved a chair in front of the middle window, and plugged the drill into the socket just below. Wrapping the tool in a towel would dampen the noise to a hum. She moistened and fastened a small suction unit onto the pane and cut a fifteen-square-inch portal from the window, the diamond chip crosscut blade almost silently cutting through the eighth-inch-thick safety glass. A cube of windowpane easily came away. So long as the room remained darkened, no one would spot the square of missing glass on the exterior window of suite 4783, forty-seven stories in the sky.

She turned the table sideways and pushed it across the rug toward the window, till the tabletop flushed up even with the bottom of the hole cut in the window. She pulled the sock covering the camouflaged suppressor. Then carefully removed the olive dapple CheyTac M200—an elegant synergy of the sinister and the beautiful—jutting from the golf bag, and slowly set it up on the table. Inserted the seven-round magazine. Adjusted the bipod so she could shoot straight through the hole in the window, the tip of the suppressor several inches back from the breach.

A quick scan with the laser rangefinder gauged the distance to the adjacent tower at 308 feet. She fed the information into the handheld ballistic computer, calibrated the scope, and sat stock-still in the darkness. Her body keenly looked, listened, sensed.

The faint scent of the carnation recalled to her the feminine, gracefully embodied by Nina Lobkovskaya, who, seventy-four years before, had joined the Red Army at seventeen. This blonde, merciless mentor—who had pink-misted over 300 heads by the age of twenty—was very much on her mind.

So was her target, who always thought he was better, smarter. That she never knew about his cruel indiscretions. Her only misgiving was that, shortly past dawn, he would rise as he always did, would drink a cup of coffee, peering out the window, taking his measure of the new day—and would never feel a thing.

As morning spread over the far tower in The City That Never Sleeps, life became pure and simple. She chambered a .408 round. The view from behind a sniper's rifle was like no other on earth.

OUT PAST GEOMETRY

We're in our work clothes, I keep telling myself. *Ready for the day shift. Nothing unusual.*

The tech slots the helmet onto my suit. Twists it a quarter turn. *Click.* The vacuum seals and I get that first blast of pure oxygen. But I'm mostly holding my breath, till Mission Control gives the word: "It's a go, gentlemen."

We muscle up to our feet, three bloated snowmen. Clammy palms. Hearts pounding. We totter down the hall. Then outside. Crawling through a sea of spectators, and finally into the van.

I match my glove to a man's hand pressed against the window. Could be any man. Any person on Earth. All of us part of something so big we can't get our heads around how it will possibly work. I've only learned how to operate my tiny part of it.

Into the open cage elevator, rising alongside the rocket that's snorting, wheezing, straining against the launch pad, with a tension building for years.

Onto the scaffolding and out the skywalk. Gaze over the ocean and blue coast. This living stuff we'll soon leave behind . . . commit it all to memory.

Slither into the command module. Strap in.

"Godspeed," says the launch captain. The hatch slams shut. This is not the simulator.

"Two minutes and counting . . ."

We're sitting on half a million gallons of kerosene and liquid oxygen. And just about now, the launch director's going to light it.

"Liftoff . . ."

The thrust mashes us back in our seats. We rattle and roar through the clouds and my eyes gape through the small window, searching for Paulina, who, every night during high school, was wheeled out to the porch by her dad and propped behind a Sears & Roebuck telescope. Paulina with "the palsy," who speaks funny but who I grew up around so could understand fine.

"Michael. You go up there. Out of this world. For both." Paulina's watching.

We peer out the small window as the blue planet rounds out below. We can't see "Texas," or the "United States." Just the land they occupy on the blue planet, with the flickering orange dots across north Africa. The scattered campfires of Bedouin nomads, Houston tells us. I want to trade places, to see us through their eyes. And for our fellow nomads to see their fires from our ship.

Everything floats. Weightless. Do I really know where I am at this point in time and space, and in reality and existence? We're hurtling through space but sense no movement. "Here" is nothing but now. "There" was, or will be.

What does "Day 3" mean up here? We watch the planet turn. No strings holding it up. Moving in a blackness which has no end and no referent.

Everything I know—humanity, people, family, love, life, green trees, and fresh water. It's all down on that bright blue dot. Not much in the black vastness. Yet the world to me.

If any of our systems go down, we'll never make it back. We're a hundred and fifty thousand miles from home. The moon comes in a flash.

We slingshot into our lunar orbit. Neil and Buzz wiggle back into their spacesuits, into the lunar module, and drop free.

I never knew how big the command module was till the other boys had gone. Wish the damn lunar module would hold three people, but the orbital rendezvous requires pilots in both ships. We don't talk much about it, but part of my training is going back alone.

My mind races. I can't slow it down.

I take a sleeping pill and dream about the blackness. And coming across a ship like ours. Inside I find the three of us, who've been up here for thousands of years. Faces glued to the small window. Our eyes without color. Clear as water.

I break from the dark side of the moon, back into the light. I'm not an astronaut flying the command module. I'm an Army brat, born in Rome. Squinting against a brighter sun than anyone has ever seen. And a blacker-than-blackness sky. A blue marble we call Earth burns far, far in the distance.

Nobody ever remembers the second person to do anything. I'm the first to be right here, so going back with some relatable feeling seems as crucial as hauling home another rock, which Neil and Buzz are collecting, down on the lunar surface.

I'm lucky to take this all in. To return knowing the presence we're experiencing in all this austerity. Beneath all feeling. A sense we are not alone. Maybe because so many on Earth are focusing their attention up here.

I hope Paulina's still watching. She imagined all this ages ago. When I was playing JV basketball and gunning a Vespa around Steubenville.

What is home but familiar things? Should we pull this off, what shall I think and feel, looking back at the moon? This unbelievably beautiful, naked, charcoal ball where we've lived. Where Neil and Buzz explored the mountains and the valleys. Living down there for days and nights as I circled at a distance, dreaming for eons.

—based on For All Mankind *(c. 1989), a documentary film made of original footage from NASA's Apollo program. Directed by Al Reinert. Music by Brian Eno.*

UNREALISTIC

a dribble

In 1920 Paris, an American GI who saw Marc Chagall's first exhibition told the artist he didn't care for modern paintings because they weren't realistic. "What do you like?" asked Chagall, and the soldier showed him a wallet photo of his girlfriend. "*Der'mo!*" said Chagall. "Is she *really* that small?"

LIBERTY
·IN·GOD·WE TRUST
1954

HAUNTED

Soon as I saw Latasha at the dance, cutting up with others in the A Group, I started plotting my ambush.

I lived on campus but always went surfing on weekends, till Hurricane Leandro locked us down. So that morning I smoked a blunt and jogged through the rain to a dance in the cafeteria. A daytime shindig organized on the spot because much of Florida was flooding, and we had nowhere to go.

The dance began with maybe sixty of us drawing numbers from a pork pie hat, dividing us into two groups. Everyone in Latasha's group (A) received a silver dollar and a blindfold. Before each song, Group A pulled on the blindfold and slow-danced with the first person who approached them. The person wearing the blindfold couldn't speak, and their partner couldn't speak.

Any student from Group A who felt something stir, an animal attraction or whatever, could gift their silver dollar to their mysterious partner. The psych department had run this social experiment several times, and what a riot to see the gawkiness on students' faces who occasionally discovered their coins in enemy hands. Latasha Coleman was my enemy, and I was hers.

The second Latasha pulled on her blindfold, I raced over and grabbed her hand, ready to squeeze till her knuckles cracked. But she smelled good, so I didn't. I could still tromp on her feet as the music started, but she flushed up close and I floated on a cloud. We hit the refrain; I leaned my head on her shoulder, feeling like a ball of light, and she put her hand on my head. When the dance ended, before she peeled of her blindfold, she handed me her silver dollar and I ran for it, getting soaked dashing back to my puny dorm room. I plunked down in my one shitty chair that I stole from the rec center. What was I thinking? Compared to Latasha Coleman, Hurricane Leandro was a breeze.

The fuse got lit months before, during the third or fourth session of Contemporary American Fiction. We were going over something I'd written, when Latasha says she never wastes time reading cis-gendered white guys' work anymore. All of us wrote meaningless dross, were narcissistic, extraneous, boring as hell, blah blah blah. The fact that I might disagree betrayed my entitlement. All our encounters fed the same toxic bonfire because we both were out to prove something.

That knocking on my door, like some farmer chopping wood, had to be Latasha. One of her friends must have outed me. Her parka streamed water when I opened the door.

"Just like you to up and run off like that," she said.

"I don't feel like doing this. Again."

"You gonna leave me standing out here?"

She sat in the plastic chair. I sat on the bed, not a yard between us.

"You enjoy tormenting me, don't you?" I said.

"So it's all about you?" she said. "You're pathetic."

I got her lousy silver dollar and told her to beat it. She batted my hand away.

"Listen to you, giving orders again. And whatever you want is what the world owes you. You know how crazy that sounds to the rest of us?"

"That's not a question," I said. "It's a setup."

"You wanna be relevant, you meet people halfway. It ain't your fucking plantation, Colonel." That felt vicious. My face was on fire. Her fuming was also my fault, apparently. "I hate your guts but I don't want to."

"Bull. Shit," I said. "You tell me I got nothing to say worth hearing, before I even speak. You profile people like that, don't expect them to like it. Or you."

We glared, cultivating our hatred like hot house flowers. Only when Latasha was blind as a bat had we escaped our mutual suspicion. Sure, some sins of my fathers might never be made right. But how were we honoring the past by letting it hold us hostage like that? Especially when those sins were limiting my options. I hated that I couldn't have it all. Which is exactly what Latasha said: it was all about me. That was the problem.

I stepped over and gazed out my one small window. Outside, wind whipped the rain sideways.

"It's like we're stuck in some shitty old house," I said. "Roof leaks, toilets back up, lights don't work. Not really our doing, but we were born here and we can't change it with some silver dollar."

"Nice try, but it's not exactly true," she said. "You own the house, remember."

"So now I'm a slum lord." I flopped back on the bed and looked at the paint peeling off the ceiling. "I can't win here, Latasha, because the game we're playing is rigged."

"It shouldn't be a game," she said. "But you make it that way so you can dominate. It wears me out."

Our moment of bliss had dissolved like sunny days. She sat there, a broken arrow. It wasn't all on me, but it might as well have been.

"Say we stop 'playing.' What would that even look like?"

"You better mean that," she said.

"Show me a way that leaves both of us standing, and maybe I'm in."

She grabbed the silver dollar off the bed and said, "I gave this to you because I thought you were somebody else . . ." But she couldn't finish her thought. "Don't blame me if I don't trust you," she finally said.

"Who do we trust, then? Or do we just keep circling the drain like this?"

Latasha went to my desk, flipped on my little transistor radio, and spun the dial past the weather reports till she landed mid-line in a ballad.

We sat there, rain drilling the window, us mouthing words, glancing off each other as Sara Vaughn sang divinely. But we were too skinned, too love sick to dance. Finally, Latasha set the silver dollar on my bed, and left.

When stormy weather hits these days, I sometimes dig out the old coin and hold it in my hand until it smolders like a meteor.

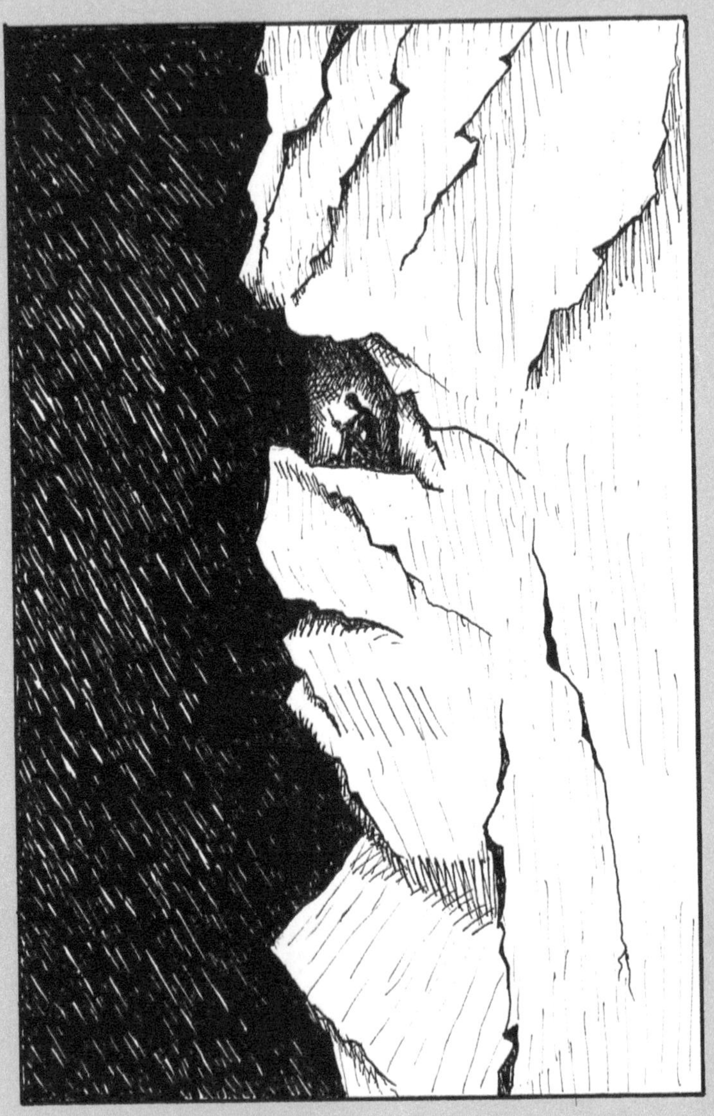

SHIVA

For a decade, maybe two, whenever David swooped into mind, I shoved him back to the blue yonder because all I could hear was dirt raining off his coffin. Then the piano plinking in his mother's house, once the *shiva* began. The black ribbon, ripped in two, lay on the dining room table. Candles burned. All the mirrors were covered.

The Rabbi kept glancing at Nate and me, but what could he say? His nephew, David, the irrepressible prodigy who went rogue on the big rocks in Yosemite and the wildest rivers on Earth, had gone where the light never shines.

Caterers ghosted through the house, carrying trays of blintzes. We couldn't stomach food so we drank coffee from a big chafer urn, the eyes of the gathering crowd playing over us—graciously, when met. But who were we? Finally the Rabbi led us up some stairs to a small room full of books and paintings, a couch, and a big desk. The former study, I imagined, of David's father, a history professor at UC Fresno, who'd passed away years before. David never said when or how because once he hit that first big rapid, his life ran ahead of him—till a moving van t-boned his Ford Pinto, and all we had of David was the past.

David's mother sat behind the desk and smiled, but couldn't hold it. David's kid sister, teetering close by her mother, drew raw, ragged breaths. It might have helped us all had she screamed.

"Truth is," said the Rabbi, "we haven't seen much of David these last five or six years." The room seemed to swallow his words. "There's a lot to be proud of. Or so we've heard."

"We're not sure who David became," the mother finally said, looking at Nate, squirming in the excruciating space David left behind. It was now Nate's job to try and fill it. Nate hadn't said a word on the two-hour drive down from Yosemite.

"Whatever you might tell us—" said the Rabbi.

Nate gazed at the desktop, arrayed with magazines and catalogues, each showing David on the cover. Mostly kayaking shots.

"Couple years ago," said Nate, "I got the wise idea to solo the North Face of Sentinel. No rope. Night before, I tell David to keep an eye on me, and he hands me a little walkie-talkie he borrowed from the rescue cache. I can't be lugging needless stuff up that wall, but David says, 'You're taking it.' So I did. I set off at five the next morning, with a bullet pack, a quart of water, a couple energy bars, and that stupid walkie-talkie.

"There's a good ledge a thousand feet up," said Nate, skipping ahead, "but I'm going so good I don't stop, and never see the sky graying over. Hour later, I'm 1,500 feet up the wall, charging for the summit, when the first big drops bomb down. Then the rock's pouring water. I burrow back into the chimney. To wait it out. The rain turns to sleet, then snow. It's dark and butt-cold. I've only got sweatpants and a fleece sweatshirt. I'm shivering like crazy.

No way I'll last till morning. By midnight I just want it over. Then David calls on the walkie-talkie."

"Because he'd been watching you up there," the sister cut in. "Just like you asked him to."

"Of course he was," said Nate. "And soon as it starts snowing, he bolts up the trail and scrambles up Sentinel Gulley, just left of the cliff. Takes him hours to reach the ridge, which is all glazed over. And his headlamp's no good in the storm. Somehow he traverses over to the top of Sentinel and hunkers under a boulder, maybe two hundred feet above me. When his voice cracks over the walkie-talkie, I think I'm hearing stuff. So I don't respond till David starts yelling at me to wake up. I'm hypothermic. Convulsive shivers. We both know if I drift off, I'm done for. But the batteries are half-dead on the walkie-talkies, so David only talks a few seconds at a go. Every twenty minutes. Screaming at me not to quit. I wanna give up but he won't stop calling. I tell him to leave me alone. He yells it. 'Wake up, you fuck!' And it goes like that till dawn, and David can get down to me on a rope."

David's mom stared at one of the magazines. Then she looked up at Nate and said, "David always told me: 'If ever I go missing, find Nate.' I'm grateful to you, Nate."

The Rabbi had driven up to Yosemite the previous evening to tell Nate about the accident, and was much obliged that we'd driven down for the service. He walked us down to the street and Nate and I piled into his beater van, the Rabbi pausing beside the open driver's side window.

"You know," said the Rabbi, "I heard that story before. But the way David told it, he got stuck up on that big rock, and you went up and got him." He handed Nate a plastic bag and said, "Something for the drive."

Nate passed me the bag and we rolled off. Not till we cleared Fresno and were driving up the 41 for Yosemite did I check the bag.

It was full of blintzes and a little bag of weed, probably found on David's person, when they cut him from his Pinto with the Jaws of Life. We still didn't feel like food, but we smoked the weed.

ABUELITA ESPERANZA

Abuelita Esperanza was twenty-three in the old black-and-white photo, sitting on the couch in her polka dot, sleeve-tie dress, a string of faux pearls around her neck, reading *London Life*, and flashing that smile that made birds bob their heads when they walk. It's the only keepsake I still have of the woman who raised me. Nothing in that photo hints that a few years later, she'd lose everything but my mom, Estella, and her second daughter, my Aunt Roberta, a writer who gave me my first bicycle.

Abuelita had just turned thirty-seven when I was born, which put her at forty-three when Mom took off with a Merchant Marine. Abuelita had an eighth-grade education and worked as an assistant accountant for Stater Brothers. She read a book every couple days. She liked Elizabeth Bowen most of all, maybe because of my Irish grandfather. We lived in a rent-controlled duplex over by the Penmar golf course, and Abuelita gave me the big room when I turned thirteen. The thing I remember most is how she'd walk into a home or an office and everyone would light right up and feel glad to be alive. She'd have turned eighty years old today. In the leaflet from her services at St. Clements, a poem read:

Amé, fui amado, el sol acarició mi faz.
¡Vida, nada me debes! ¡Vida, estamos en paz!

(I loved, I was loved, the sun caressed my face.
Life, you owe me nothing. Life, we are at peace.)

Happy Birthday, Grandma Esperanza. *Te amo siempre.*

TO HAVE AND TO HOLD

Selkie tells me to get in her car, and she'll hear no guff. I've promised to marry Selkie when I return from Yemen in a couple months. Teresa, my neighbor, will preside. That was the plan, declared last Christmas, after the eggnog and Thai weed brownies, and I'd hoped Selkie had forgotten all about it. She hasn't.

She drives us down by the Getty Villa and we walk out onto the beach. I've been drinking beer like water and haven't jogged much or lifted weights, as usual. Selkie can tell. I need a haircut and haven't shaved. Selkie mentions this. She bought me those nice shirts, so why aren't I wearing one? I look fubared, and she won't hear me lie or make excuses. But how am I? Really?

I go to answer and Selkie keeps asking me about my work, which she knows little about. Am I scared about my next assignment? Am I still meditating, like I promised? Do I love my life? Love her? "You better . . ." Every word strung out that little bit further as she slows me down till we are just two people walking along the seashore. She pulls me shin-deep into the surf.

We're not like the others, she says. Too many acute angles. Too quirky. So we drift out to deep waters. Alone on the ocean. She's out there too. So is her father, whose family owns hotels and who calls from Berlin when he's drunk. And always forgets her birthday.

We sit down in the sand and watch the combers. There's too much of us inside of us, says Selkie. The jinx of the outsized, who always require an audience, leaving us with each other. She's making me edgy. Like the Swiss foreign exchange girl who signed my yearbook in high school. Who knew me better than I knew myself.

Maybe, says Selkie, the waves will wash away the excess, leaving us wonderfully normal, cool and unencumbered on the sand. Even she doesn't like the idea.

I grab Selkie. If she wasn't so rich, I tell her, so hip, and so ornery, I'd almost marry her. That's just like me, she laughs, thinking the choice is mine. We're getting married the moment I return from Yemen, don't forget. I remind that our union, like a henna tattoo, has no chance of lasting. "Every concert ends," she says, rapping my chest with her knuckles, "but you still buy tickets if you like the band." She wants to experience, at least once in her life, the big bash and all the showy gifts. And for our friend Josh to jump out of the cake.

We wade out into the surf and Selkie grabs my face and kisses me, biting my lip. For a minute, I'm no longer walking the plank for Yemen, telling myself that embedded journalists always make it back.

MATHEMATICALLY IMPOSSIBLE

When Grover Cleveland's disc plow snagged on the strange object, fallen from the sky into his turnip field, he trucked it straight to Sterling, his oldest boy, who interned at the scientific institute in Cambridge.

Summer session had let out and even Dr. Ennis Dinkwater, the Lab Director, was still on vacation. Only Sterling and Paisley, another grad student, remained in the lab—an arrangement that poached Sterling's apples for months, as he imagined the kinematic ways he and Paisley might integrate propulsions and corroborate his theory.

Sterling scanned the strange object with dopplers. Paisley drilled it with gluon splitters. What could it be?

Leonardo, fetched from Geophysics, gauged the strange object for God particles, and said, "Not mineral. Certainly off-world."

Moses, arrived from Engineering, bombed the strange object with pre-solar grains and fissile ball-peens. Not a scratch on the strange object.

When Annabelle, Decibel Tech at the Acoustics Laboratory,

blasted the strange object with binomial infrasound, they had such a sonic jamboree going on, Moses feared they'd disrupt the stratosphere.

The strange object glowed, hiccupped, swole, and spontaneously morphed into a clump of shock-blue goo, like the Slime so prized by kids.

"Freaking shapeshifter," said Sterling. "Read about those."

"But what, exactly, is shifting shapes?" asked Maverick, dropped in from the Bio Lab. He ran a quick pyrogenic analysis and declared, "It's not biological. Not as natural science understands it."

Lorraine, from Audio/Visual, rigged a neutronic video camera feeding an atomic resolution big screen.

Shockingly, incomprehensibly, the goo began growing, not by dividing and multiplying through granular proliferation, as anything living must do. Rather, the glob simply increased in resting mass, without growing additional parts.

"That's mathematically impossible," said Jefferson, there from the Strict Equations Lab. "A prime number cannot increase in 'size' and remain the same number."

Sterling didn't follow. Meanwhile, Paisley took hold of the pulsing glob of goo, kneading it as the baker works the loaf.

"It's morphing," warned Maverick, studying the neutronic video.

Paisley jerked her hands away. "It bit me!"

Then—jumping zygots! An exact clone of Paisley, entirely naked, stood boldly atop the lab stand, looking distant as its head cleared.

"It metabolized your DNA from the skin on your hands," Maverick whispered, staring at the clone. "A perfect replica."

Paisley, mortified, drew closer, as Moses scanned the clone's neuronal topography with a Johnson Rod. Then he waved the rod over Paisley's skull.

"Not a replica," said Moses. "You two are identical, in every way."

"Two points variously distributed cannot be the same points," said Jefferson.

"They're entangled," said Annabelle.

"That's not me!" said Paisley, glaring at her doppelganger.

"Sure looks like you," said Sterling, grinning dumbly at the clone.

Paisley stepped between the two. "Quit staring, you perv, and get something to pull over it."

"It?" said the clone. "Try *her,* sister."

"I'm not your sister!" said Paisley.

"More than sisters," said Maverick, scanning the readout on the Johnson Rod. "She's even got your memories."

Paisley blanched. Sterling offered his lab coat, which the clone slipped into handsomely. She took Sterling's hand and stepped off the lab stand, thanking him with whetted eyes.

Paisley drew close to the clone, shook her finger, and said, "Don't go there. You know he's some hayseed stumbled in from a turnip patch."

"Tastes differ," said the clone, sidling alongside Sterling.

"I agitate the cross-linked promethium and he hovers," said Paisley. "I enrich the cosmitron and he leers. It's so annoying. How can you forget that?" Paisley stepped back and paused, gathered herself, and said, "Gawd. The most shocking discovery in the history of life science, and I'm going on about boys?"

"I'm telling you," said the clone, "we've got lives to lead."

"It's my life and you're not living it," Paisley snapped.

"And you are?" asked the clone, tapping its forehead, teeming with Paisley's recollections. "Binge-watching *The Real Housewives of Cassiopeia*. Sneaking one in with the quantum mechanic."

"I came first!" Paisley screamed.

"If you're exactly the same," said Annabelle, "what does 'first' possibly mean?"

"It's academic," said Maverick. Then everyone started yelling over themselves, flapping their arms.

"Get me outta here," the clone said to Sterling.

Paisley jumped between the two.

"You can't take that . . . *thing*, out of this lab!" Paisley said, glaring at Sterling.

Sterling grinned stupidly. "Watch me."

They didn't return till the following afternoon, finding Paisley alone, pacing in her Doc Martens. Sterling looked like he'd jogged to Manitoba and back. His telling grin at the clone—blowzy in her scarlet, backless slip dress—crucified Paisley.

"Whatever you did with that . . . *thing*," said Paisley, fuming like ammonium, "you didn't do it with me!"

"Relax, girl," said the clone. "You like the mechanic, remember? Not Molly and Johnny Walker." And she winked at Sterling.

Paisley grabbed Sterling's arms, beseeching. "She's evil, Sterling. And she's playing you like a tambourine. Can't you see that?"

"How would I know," said Sterling. "I'm just some hayseed stumbled in from a turnip patch."

Paisley wheeled toward the clone, and said, "You! You've hoodwinked the farm boy!"

Paisley snatched the Johnson Rod off the zircon calipers, wielding it like a cricket bat. The clone lunged and wrestled free the Rod, which fell to the ground. They dervished around, grabbing at the other till they clasped each other's hands, fingers interlaced. Both jerked and shimmied as their eyes rolled; and Paisley poured out of herself, like phosphate from a beaker, into a mound of blue goo.

“Quick,” said the clone. “She’ll reconstitute in minutes.”

Sterling foisted the mound into a wide-mouth grip jar and the two, as planned, hustled over to maintenance, where Sterling pitched the jar into the blast furnace. The shrieking of a thousand hyenas rose above rushing flames. Then nothing but blue tendrils lofting from the stacks as the two scurried back to the lab.

The clone grabbed Paisley’s purse and jacket from her locker.

“Where *you* going?” asked Sterling.

“Gotta drop by my place and freshen up,” she said, shoving a dust mop into Sterling’s hands. “Better tidy up the place, farmboy. Dinkwater’s back this afternoon.”

SOUL TRAVELER

We heard Desirae sing at the Newport Jazz Festival. Forty years ago. A lean Black girl in a blue sundress, maybe twenty, guileless as rain. *Dark Moon, The Man I Love, Tears in my Heart*. She made these songs her own and took us to Andromeda, to the warmest pocket of our being. And to Land's End. Reminding us acutely of our long lost, with a grace surpassing all sorrows. Up and gone when the music ended. All Bill Evans, her pianist, ever heard was that she'd moved to South Carolina shortly after the gig. Arrived from nowhere. Never seen before, nor after. This soul traveler, Desirae, who took a piece of all of us with her when she left.

A LEGIT HARDBODY

She couldn't spoof me with her gaberdine slacks and ruffled lace blouse. Even with the big paisley mask covering her face, I knew it was her. The raven beehive rising off her head, with the wiggly blonde stripes on the side. The rapier eyebrows. The dimple in her chin. And the incisions—faded to thin stenciled lines—running under her neck, where Herr Frankenstein had stitched the Bride together. We were in the way-back on a near-empty connector to Missoula. What were the odds?

Once airborne, she spun from the window seat and barked, "Quit staring. It's rude."

"Sorry," I said. "Name's Figaro." She stifled a laugh and I said, "Yeah. Like the *Barber of Seville*. Don't start in on me too."

"I know the feeling," she said, softening a little. "I'm Wendy."

I expected Frida, or maybe Ursula.

"Gotta say, you don't look a day over thirty," I said, "for being . . . what, like a hundred?"

"Hundred and seventeen. But I'm paleo and exercise like a heptathlete. Look."

She held out her arm and I squeezed. The Bride of Frankenstein was a legit hardbody.

"Hold up for a second," I said. "The way I remember it, the monster thought you all should die. So he pulls the lever and the castle blows up. You, the monster, the doctor—"

"The doctor perished," she said. "But Bernhard—that's the bully's name—he and I escaped out the dungeon."

"Your boy Bernhard's got a dozen lives," I said. "First the windmill burns—"

"He's not my boy," she said. "I loathe the galoot from here to eternity."

"Sorta got that," I said. "You screaming at him in the movie—"

"Who's he to decide I should die like that? Repulsive big lummox with a groundhog's brain."

"Not the friendliest decision," I said. "Come to think—"

"Guys don't have women as 'friends,'" she cut in, "'cause they're not. It's a truism."

"It's rubbish. My best friend in college was a female."

"How many kids do you have now?"

"Two," I said. "But I still have female friends, besides the wife. A stack of them."

"And every one you find attractive is a fuck buddy hopeful," she said. "Don't think she doesn't know that. And most of us gals with a posse of guy pals have friend-zoned them as backups, in case Wolfgang skips with the hot yoga instructor." She whisked the air with her hand. "You know those friendships usually blow up, then the guy gets sore. Or crazy."

"You're dark," I said.

"I'm right," she said. "Why do you think I'm flying into Podunk, Montana? Because Bernhard's been stalking me since World War II. Okay, we had a little spree in Baton Rouge, during the armistice, when everyone felt giddy—"

"Must have been an adventure when you buttered the biscuit," I said.

"He smelled like jambalaya," she said. "He's vigorous. I'll give him that. But he never got past that weekend. That's seventy-five years ago!" She paused as the rancor roared through. "I can't even watch the geyser in Yellowstone without the big oaf racing up in his stupid truck. He's dogged me to Niagara, the Everglades. Even to the carnival down in Rio. I'm over it."

The flight attendant announced we'd soon land in Missoula.

The Bride pulled off her mask, heaved a sigh, and said, "And I'm over this COVID crap as well. These lockdowns have cost me bank. Over a damn cold." She clenched the mask in her fist. "This thing is so annoying."

Jeepers. The Bride was one of those nutters full of horse de-wormer and conspiracy theories. Unvaccinated for sure. And I'd sat next to her for forty-five minutes.

"If that mask is bugging you," I said, "you're gonna hate the ventilator."

She ignored me and frantically keyed her iPhone. The second we deplaned, the Bride, running the wheels off her carry-on, dashed through the small airport to the pick-up area out front, dove into a waiting Lyft, and wheeled out onto the 12, motoring toward Seely Lake.

I fetched my checked bag and wandered out to the street, thinking that half-wit hunchback had gone and purloined a loopy brain for the Bride as well. The Bride had some truth in her, but it came roaring out sideways, much as the big Dodge 4x4 that yawed to a stop, nearly running over my desert boots.

A giant jumped out. Wolverine hikers. Blue jeans. Harvard Rugby jersey. The red beanie pulled over his head couldn't disguise his anvil-flat pate. It was him alright. Bernhard. The monster. He stormed over, shoved a cell phone into my face with a recent photo of him and the Bride at a luau over in Kauai, both looking fly in Aloha shirts and orchid leis.

"You seen this woman?" he asked.

"Just sat next to her on the jet plane," I told him. "Said you've been stalking her from hell and back."

"Of course she did. Old battle-axe filches my debit card and drains my savings. Third time it's happened, I swear."

Guy must have gotten into a program or something, because he sounded nothing like he did in the old talkies. I thought he might weep, like when he heard the blind old duffer sawing that violin during the first film. I put a hand on his knobby shoulder; he slouched down on the curb and I plopped down beside him, a couple feet away.

"Let her go," I said. "Cut your losses. People like her make fools out of people like us."

He lit a smoke and gazed out at Big Sky country, dusted with snow. "Like we need any help doing that."

CHUCKING LEMONS

"No one ever accused me of being smart," said the rockstar. "Hell, I'd run to all the tight spots for the thrill of busting out. Still do."

The short Instagram vid consisted of one continuous, shaky take, shot on an Air Bus, so I could barely make out his words.

"We used to tromp to the other side of this lemon grove near my house," he went on, "where it ended at a street, and we'd chuck lemons at cars. We hear a *Bam!* and squealing tires. We'd run like crazy, hoping someone good and pissed off was chasing after."

I could hear this delinquent bedlam in the rocker's iconic songs—always loved his stuff—as he rubbed the magic lantern of his old pranks.

"Sorry about the dents, all you peoples—you know who you are. Was never about trashing your car, but getting you to chase after. So we could make the mad dash, with something closing fast that could ruin us. That feeling . . ." He grinned, remembering.

But the grin went upside down, recalling how his scattered kid self, barely twenty-two and already filling stadiums, went gonzo rebel, having no one but himself to seek revenge. All that blow and booze. The serial *amores* and fractured promises. Until, half mad and broke, all he had left was that feeling. He looked at the camera and said, "What was the question again?"

The woman shooting the vid chuckled behind her iPhone, and said, "I asked how you wrote all those songs?" They were several bourbons into a transatlantic flight.

"Song writing's hard," he said. "And I fancied hard. My poor mum went broke looking for hard things to hook me, so I didn't land in HMYOI—Her Majesty's Young Offender Institution. Like juggling, card tricks, bongo boards—broke my ass on one. Come Christmas, she buys me a unicycle. I jump on board and it feels totally impossible. I'm hooked. Took me ages to ride ten feet with a hand on the wall. When the wall ends and I try riding off, I fall on my face for days. Then one time I just ride off. Felt wild as running through the lemon grove. Week later, I'm riding the thing to school, so now I need something else. Something harder. So my mom bought me a used guitar. Old Squire Strat. Played it at Wembley last year."

"How old were you?" she asked. "When she bought you the Strat?"

"I think—twelve," said the rockstar. "Everything on the guitar felt hard, which made me practice like mad, trying all this gymnastic fingering. Carried me through music school, then onto the road to start gigging. And writing songs. Push the chorus into chaos for a sec, then try to resolve it. Hard nut to crack, but when I could, it felt dope as riding the uni off the wall. Rocking the big gigs—those are like running through the grove. Like you're all going to hell, but you might stay alive for one more set—if you play with all your might."

The woman laughed again and said, "You still haven't said why you wrote all those songs."

The rocker shrugged and said, “Keep from throwing lemons at cars, I guess. And binging. Can’t run like I used to, but I still love havoc, and the electronic guitar . . . thanks to Mum.”

SELAMA LEMANYA

We traveled up a river that had no name, heading for a green alp in the jungled highlands. The river curved into a shady vestibule where the hardwood trees came down to the water line and the canopy nearly blocked out the sun. In a clearing on the left-hand bank, under a ramin tree arching over the river, a small, slat-sided hut perched on palm pylons. We motored down and glided onto a gravel bar. Our last sight of human life lay three days and two tributaries behind us.

A young woman walked from the jungle, leading a naked girl toddler with one hand and dragging a big, ripe jackfruit in the other. Near sundown, the woman's husband pulled ashore in a hand-hewn, motorized dugout. He invited us inside the hut.

Seamus dug out some shag tobacco and we smoked huge cigarettes rolled from pages of a paperback I had in my pack. One of our group spoke Bahasa, and we learned that, for five years, the couple had panned gold from a network of creeks nearby. Recently, they had tickled out fortune enough to move back to Bandung and do most anything they chose. Even buy a car. But they had no plans to leave. They would stay there on the riverside, *selama lamanya* (forever). The woman fried some rice and we rustled up guavas and alligator pears. Then the man invited us to follow him, and for nearly two hours, we walked upstream along the river, feeling more than seeing our way. The sky burned with stars, but there was no moon and the closing jungle was dark and the lazy river black as ink. The man stopped and swam out into the river; we followed, and rolling onto our backs, let the cool, delicate current carry us along. We floated through the night. Nobody said a word. On both sides, the banyans rose in the black decor.

Back in the hut, as we prepared for sleep, the man tapped out his pipe and said that, when the day came that he found himself old and tired, he would make amends to Allah and wait for night to fall. He would have a last meal of rice and durian fruit, and would say goodbye to his family. Then he would wade out into the river and drift with the current. He would not swim to shore. He would just keep on going. *Selama lamanya.*

I'M LIQUOR

Of course I saw you saunter in. Style with attitude is required in Apollo's Lair, but not such timeless elegance. Holy Ghost, just look at you, in your fitted, mauve, one-shoulder silhouette dress. Who else makes such a grand gesture, simply by sitting down?

We are destined to be soul mates. Nobody understands, or sees you like I do. Your annoying insecurities . . . Not to worry. I'll wash them all away in nothing flat. So no one else will know. And likewise, *mi amor*—I'm pleased to meet you, I'm sure.

I'm Black Rat and Witty Chuck. I'm Goof, I'm Booze, I'm Giggle Juice. I'm the Slayer of Fear. I'm Mother's Ruin. I'm Liquor.

Okay. Crashing your Lexus is regrettable. Truly. Of course it was an accident, and the DUI was unfair. Four measly mimosas? I understand you never pictured yourself in county jail. And sorry about getting crabs from the blanket. But you're free now, so quit being so sensitive. You need a little distance, to get perspective. Relax and regroup. Let's pull together on this. Pool our resources. You and me. I'm here for you.

I'm Rifleman. I'm Who-Shot-John. I'm The Water of Life, and

Flirtini. I'm Blow Hole, Pop Skull, Goldidrunk, and Ruckus. I'm Sunshine in a Bottle. I'm Liquor.

You don't know what you're talking about. Bitch-slapping the branch manager was not my fault. I mean, how's that about me when you did it? No. I never said: Have another. You're remembering it wrong. Where do you come up with this stuff? I'm not angry, but you have to change. And you have to appreciate who your real friends are. Especially me.

I'm Nelson's Blood. I'm Skinny Captain. I'm Uncle Carl and Voon. I'm Green Gimble and Pink Ginade. White Satin and Blue Ruin. I'm Droolaid. I'm Liquor.

Damn right you're an alcoholic. Because you don't *respect* me. You're lucky I put up with you. Look around. Nobody wants to be around you. You're not a team player. You're a miserable, petty, party of one. Incompetent and unteachable. Remember that dust-up in rehab? Shows how broken you are. How anxious and jealous. And crazy. I knew that going in, but I stuck with you anyhow, because even you deserve a friend. Someone staunch and loyal. And right now, princess, I'm all you've got.

You're Paralytic, Rat-Arsed, Plastered, Railed, and Ploughed. You're Shit-Faced, Shit-Housed, Slammered and Squiffy. Jiggered, Gobsmacked, Gone. I'm Liquor.

Big deal that you've gone without me for twenty days. You tried that, what—a dozen times? Ever since I lit your fuse back at Apollo's Lair. Was it really sixteen years ago?

You were so tormented. Pie-eyed porch climber, roostering around in your kitschy dress. The vanity. I could disclose things about you. And what do you mean, that pleasing me was killing you? You're a liar and a cheat. You're all charades.

You only say you've decided to walk away. Girl, I've heard that for centuries, from kings and guttersnipes. Wait till you get fired again. When he's had enough and the money's gone. When sleep won't come and the black hole in your belly swallows you whole. You'll come crawling on hands and knees. Your thankless kind always come back. Or try and white-knuckle it—longing, dreaming, mouth-watering for me. Admit it. You need me. Your bestie for life.

I'm Slim-Jim Slammerson, Mockingbird, and The Devil's Vomit. I'm Yak Potion, Lantern Fuel, Heartbreak's Helper, and Felony Juice. I'm Liquor.

NO MAN'S LAND

Just after her twenty-second birthday, with heedless abandon, Dawn slid onto the back of a Vespa and her boyfriend gunned it down Pacific Coast Highway—and right off the road. He stumbled away with road rash and a busted arm. Dawn rag-dolled into a barranca.

A tide of morphine swept her through the UCLA Trauma Unit. She crashed again in rehab. Rattling off opioids. Screaming her way through physical therapy, hoping for "a miracle." It never came. She couldn't spiritually survive, stuck in the body she had.

She loved light verse, but the words felt unreachable after her accident. So she wished upon the first book she grabbed: Jack London's *Klondike Tales,* where a throng of young have-nots leaped into the Klondike gold rush and stormed through the frozen Yukon. Every soul seeking fortune in Alaska, a place so big and wild it could rewrite you. London didn't so much tell stories as he told his life—a life she desperately needed.

She spent many nights exploring the intrigues, a century before, surrounding the first ascent of Denali, the highest mountain in North America. Watching Alutiiq war dances on YouTube. In the Alaska of her mind, she floated through Eclutna spirit houses, mushed a dog sled, "hauled herring" on a commercial fishing boat, and fell into a crevasse.

She surfed the internet and befriended mountaineers, rafters, ice cavers who described fantastic Alaskan adventures—some true—that stirred like hot mustard in the blandness of her days. Made her remember exciting people she'd never met, and dangerous places where, at some time, she must have visited yet had somehow forgotten. The anaesthetizing lies of her life.

The posts and photos poured in, year after year. From Kodiak Island and the Matanuska Glacier. From a cool blue lake under a blue, blue sky. So many stories and memories, none of them her own, and desaturating by the year. Till finally the postcards, still arriving, were colorless relics from other people's lives. She found herself where she'd been all along, sequestered in a steel gray condo in Culver City, California.

That night, she drank. That started when Karsten, a Norwegian alpinist, visited her the week before, on his way back to Anchorage to work on the Alaska Pipeline. She rarely accepted visitors; but they'd known each other, cyberly, for several years. They'd chatted, texted (he sent her a message from the top of Mount Forraker), even started Zooming when the Delta virus locked him down in Stavanger. He was laying-over right down the road at LAX.

He Ubered over and they talked. Mainly, she talked; the words gushing from her unrestrained. Karsten was that kind of listener. He wasn't bothered by her situation. And he wasn't some rescuer, because he didn't pity her.

"Everything works," he said, "but you can't walk. Is that it?"

Blood rushed to her face. A fault line ran from Pacific Coast Highway straight into that condo, and Karsten was walking the length of it. She could race him through it, editing as she wanted, but he had no right to trespass like that on his own.

"I can stand," she said, tersely. "But I'm not getting up just to prove it."

Karsten cocked his head and said, "You're still in that barranca, aren't you? That needs to change."

He didn't see a tragic figure. Only her vehement mulishness. If art is perfect empathy, Karsten was no artist. But he wanted her just the same. Hate welled off her in waves.

"You need to leave now," she said.

Her future had stretched to infinity. All the time in the world to learn new languages, to walk the Tour de Mt. Blanc in summer, to march a passel of boys, each more aching and delicious than the last, through their paces. Then time ended in that barranca.

Karsten texted her two days later: "Just buy a ticket and get up here. I'll meet you in Fairbanks with my van. We'll manage."

She never asked for what Karsten kept offering. Some lesser life. No one could make her accept that. Her finger hovered over the message for minutes before she hit DELETE.

She rolled her chair over the window and saw the lone star hanging faintly above the glaring Costco sign. Someone had recently sent her a postcard featuring Van Gogh's *Starry Night*, with a passage on the back saying the stars are the souls of dead poets. But while you're alive, you can never reach them. Can never hear their words.

Her fists clenched. To die peacefully, sitting on her ass, was like crawling for the stars on hand and foot. She wanted the bullet train, and only had her chair.

She sat in astringent solitude, resigned to a long journey, to never move again, to never drink or eat or dream of somewhere else, till a skyful of souls, finally, would haul her out of that barranca.

MURDERATION

a trecenta

It takes Everett fifteen minutes to wheedle down to First Class and find Mr. Brooks' cabin. The door flies open after the second knock.

"Believe this is yours," says Everett, handing Mr. Brooks a big leather wallet. "I found it under a lounge chair. By the shuffleboard courts, where I work."

Mr. Brooks takes his wallet and riffles the fat sheaf of bills inside. "When I was your age, I'd have kept this."

"I was tempted," says Everett. "I give it to the purser and you get the wallet back, but the money's gone. You know how that goes." Mr. Brooks chuckles. Everett says, "I better get back."

Everett goes to turn but Mr. Brooks grabs his arm and looks him over. Brooks respects the type, probably born into nothing, who, under different circumstances, might eventually run this ship. Or own it. Mr. Brooks pulls the entire sheaf of bills from his wallet and shoves them into Everett's hand.

Then a long, basso moan shudders from the starboard side of the ship. Then silence.

"Good luck to you, kid," says Mr. Brooks, and shuts the door.

Everett has never held a hundred- or a fifty-dollar bill. He counts out the wad. A fortune. "Mother of God," he mumbles. Then yells it, his voice volleying down the hallway and filling the entire ship.

He tucks the bankroll into his pocket and starts up the narrow employee staircase toward the promenade, having to turn sideways as several workers wriggle by, shouldering big bags of laundry.

"Of course I heard it," says one of the guys to the other.

"Little Joe, down in the Tank Top, says we grazed an iceberg."

"Murderation!" He sounded scared.

Everett squeezes past and continues climbing the stairs. Iceberg, smiceberg. This is the luckiest day of his life.

SHANE
MAVERICK
POWER
CORRUPTION
LIES

OLD TROPES

"No gaudy belt buckles and no denim," said Mel. "And bury the hats and cowboy boots."

"So what does our agent wear?" asked Adam.

"Not that sissy 'woke' get-up you got on." Mel chuckled. "Shane Maverick wouldn't be caught dead with all that product in his crew cut."

"I'm not some Special Investigator for the Montana Department of Justice," said Adam, referencing the lead of their unwritten series.

That wise idea belonged to Hal Pasternak, who sold the series on the strength of a one-page treatment—all concept, no details. Then COVID carried him off. The network decided to push ahead, recruiting showrunner Mel Green to build a screenwriting crew. Four of us so far, including Adam, Mel's nephew (fresh off a Nextflix series about Seattle rum runners, shitcanned after three episodes), all of us struggling to flesh out a show bible, starting with the star, rugged Montana lawman, Shane Maverick.

“We’re changing his name to Walter Garcia,” said Mel.

Dewey Holcomb, 77—Heritage boots, Wrangler jeans, big sparkly belt buckle—colleague of Hal Sloan and a western writer as well, looked at Mel like he must be joking.

“Garcia didn’t grow up with the Sioux or the Blackfoot people,” said Mel. “He’s a badminton player from Chico State. Excitable, but he never feuds or seeks revenge. And he knows that every outlaw is somebody’s son or daughter.”

Dewey Holcomb, assigned to the project “to ensure verisimilitude,” adjusted his bones and said, “Can’t says I cotton to where you’re heading with this, Melvin.”

“Give me a second. It gets better,” said Mel. “Agent Garcia doesn’t have a sacred bond with the land. The spread he doesn’t own hasn’t been in his family for five generations, so no one’s trying to swindle him out of it. And he doesn’t give a shit about horses or beeves.”

“A dog,” I said. “Montana lawmen always have dogs.”

“Little brown Maltese,” said Mel. “Call him Brutus. And he bites Garcia repeatedly.”

“Where might Agent Garcia live?” asked Rachael, a gay Miami Beach playwright and unlikely western dramatist—except she could write about anything and make it catch fire.

“Wherever it is,” said Mel, “there’s no river to go down to or shed to slink behind. No old family photographs in hand-carved frames. No adobe brick fireplace where he never chucks logs that Garcia never ever cut with an ax. And no saddle blankets on cracked leather armchairs where Garcia ponders wrongs and makes tough-but-just decisions.”

The more Dewey Holcomb squirmed, the faster Mel spoke.

“There’s no picture window,” said Mel, “where Garcia gazes out at snowy mountains and dreams about the elk he’ll shoot with a Winchester he never engraved himself. Only one thing Garcia hates more than plug tobacco and landscape paintings: guns. He's honorable, to a point; but when shots are fired, he hides behind purple sage and baby strollers because Walter Garcia takes lead for nobody."

"But he likes his whisky," said Adam. "Give us that much."

"Garcia will take a drink," said Mel. "Sure he will. But he can't hold his liquor, so he only drinks white wine. Chardonnay."

That knocking was Hal Pasternak, punching the lid on his casket.

Dewey Holcomb stood up like a heron on a drainpipe and said, "I wish y'all luck with your show, 'cause you're gonna need it." It looked as though Holcomb's ostrich-skin boots walked the old scribe right out of the room.

"You did that on purpose," I said.

"Kinda hated to," said Mel. "Ninety-five years ago, Holcomb did solid work. But we keep the old fart on now and he'd have us writing *Red River*."

"What about Walter Garcia?" said Adam.

"Never heard of him," said Mel. "So, Rachael, who's this Shane Maverick."

Rachael flipped open her daily planner and scanned a handwritten paragraph.

"Dad's a Black Arab. Mother's a Quaker from Pennsylvania. Transferred over from Homeland Security after the questionable shooting of a Juarez narco. Coming off a bad marriage, so dying to bed his partner, Babs O'Shaughnessy, a single mom with man problems. Six foot one in Hermès pumps. Just over from the DEA. Of course, they're both professionals, but by the end of episode two, Maverick's balls are blue as Lake Tahoe. But they got bigger issues: drugs flooding in from Canada. A release valve for during gray pandemic days. ODs by the hundreds. And someone in the governor's office is in on it . . ."

Mel smiled. Nobody writes their way past old tropes, or else they wouldn't be old tropes. You reject them by doubling down, diversifying the cast, updating the wardrobe, trickling out the vernacular, then call that firsthand. Welcome to show business.

"Does Maverick wear jeans?" asked Adam.

"Tight as a tiger's stripes," said Rachael. "And he loves him some Merle Haggard."

Mel pushed back from his desk, kicked his Chuck Taylors up on the table and said, "Goddamn show's gonna run forever."

MARCHING POINT

I laid over for a week in Kuwait, on my way back to Cincinnati. In most Arab countries, women walk about ten feet behind their husbands, so it surprised me to see the men, especially in rural areas, walking yards behind their wives. I wondered if this role reversal dated back to the 1990 Iraqi invasion, when many Kuwaiti men ran for their lives, while the women held their ground. A Kuwaiti woman said there had been no role reversal, or anything of the sort. Then why, I asked, were the women now marching point? "Land mines," said the woman.

REARVIEW

a drabble

Couple nights ago, I watched an old film called *Grand Prix,* starring James Garner as a world champion driver over in Europe. They're at Le Mans. A driver just died and the others are in a bar, drinking and staring at the ground. The Garner character tells a journalist how he used to see a car go up in flames and he'd feel so weak inside he wanted to stop his car and walk away. "But I'm older now," says Garner. "When I see something horrible, I put my foot down, hard, because I know everyone else is lifting theirs."

ALLIGATOR MARKETING

"What does a 750-pound alligator eat? Well, just about anything it wants," the article began, "but items found in this particular Mississippi alligator's stomach defy odds and date back better than 150 years."

Homer Renfro, owner of Blue Antler Processing in Yazoo City, Mississippi, had recently butchered a giant gator. Inside the beast's stomach, he discovered a Philadelphia Deringer, the model of pocket pistol John Wilkes Booth used to assassinate Honest Abe.

Photographs showed Dr. Wilbur Sax, of the Museum of Mississippi History, examining the pistol with a spectrograph.

The saga first began to unfold the previous April, when a wild game meat processor in South Carolina reported opening the stomach of an alligator and finding a souvenir mint julep cup from the 1964 Kentucky Derby. Homer Renfro had his doubts, but he nevertheless began examining stomach contents of the larger alligators he processed—and discovered the Philly Pocket Pistol. Soon as Homer posted his findings on Blue Antler Processing's Instagram feed, the Mississippi Clarion Ledger ran the story, which quickly went viral.

Of course, sober heads wanted to know how a 150-year-old pistol ended up inside the stomach of an alligator with a maximum lifespan of fifty years. Opinions varied, but the story got lift off and the Blue Antler site logged 350,000 hits over the following weeks. Which got Cedric "Jimbo" Bowie, of Prestige Processing—another wild game processing joint out of nearby Holy Bluff—to start conducting his own alligator autopsies.

"The shite we pull out of them gators," said Jimbo. "Like opening gifts on Christmas. Everybody standing around, waiting to see what's next. Most of it junk. Rocks. Old bottles. Even a hubcap off a Ford Edsel. Till we found this."

The photo showed a mustachioed Jimbo holding up a set of discolored dog tags dangling from a beaded chain. The dog tag, in close up, read: Hershel G. Mulroon. 22312943 T43 44 B+ Mississippi, USA.

Responses were few, till a history professor from the University of Mississippi-Oxford reminded readers (providing yellowing news clippings to boot) that Corporal Hershel G. Mulroon had received the Congressional Medal of Honor for his courageous acts during the Battle of Verdon, where the war hero was wounded and sent back home to Midnight, Mississippi. Mulroon, who had no known relatives, had left his rehab in Holy Bluff for a short piece of fishing at the Panther Swamp National Wildlife Refuge. The corporal was never seen again.

Ballads were sung, parades organized, and school holidays in Mulroon's honor continued well into the 1930s. But his disappearance was never accounted for till Jimbo Bowie found the corporal's dog tags in his killer's belly.

Web-surfing Mississippians were delighted to rediscover an old war hero. Photos and reprints of archive news articles about Hershel Mulroon ran on the Prestige Processing website, which also offered silk-screened shirts of the corporal's likeness, charging a phalanx of German soldiers with Ka-Bar clenched between his teeth.

Dissenting voices soon entered the conversation. An investigative journalist for *VICE* discovered that Homer Renfro, of Blue Antler Processing, was actually Timothy Dean Renfro, who earned a marketing degree from Ole Miss. Cedric "Jimbo" Bowie had graduated *cum laude* from University of Louisville with a history degree. Public opinion started tilting towards these faux hillbillies running promotional spoofs for their respective companies, each trying to outshine the other.

But neither campaign held a candle to Bocifus Dobbs Spaight, director of Roundoak Wild Game Processing, in nearby Ebanezer. A photo showed Director Spaight holding up a badly corroded typhoon lantern he'd carved from the belly of an Alligator mississippiensis weighing better than 1,650 pounds. Examination of the lantern by Dr. Herbert Butts, anthropology professor at Tougaloo College, established the lantern as sixteenth century, with definitive markings indicating it had arrived with the first pilgrims on the Mayflower.

"This here's a piece of history," said Bocifus Spraight on the Roundoak TikTok feed. "But the miracle ain't so much the lantern itself," Bocifus went on, in a spirited video, "rather, when I pulled it from the gator, the sumbitch was still lit!"

TO BURY HIM PROPER

We first find him in Ohio in 1801, with a mule-load of apple seeds gathered from cider presses.

"Whether impelled in his eccentricities by some misery of heart, which could only find respite through incessant motion or benevolent monomania," wrote William D'Arcy in *Harper's Magazine,* c. 1871, "his whole life was devoted to planting apple seeds in the meanest wilderness."

His seeds sprouted into buds, and vast orchards embellished the wilds, as his name grew renown in every log cabin from the Ohio River to the northern lakes and westward across the prairies of Indiana. But Johnny Appleseed was the strangest dude the pioneers had ever seen: a restless nomad with fierce eyes, forever bare-footed, with long black hair and a scraggly beard he never shaved. His primary garment was a burlap coffee sack, with holes for his head and arms. His headgear, a tin vessel that served to cook his mush.

"Thus queerly clad," wrote D'Arcy, "he perpetually wandered through forests and morasses to suddenly appear in white settlements and hostile Indian villages." The rudest frontiersmen treated him with respect. Likewise the "wild and sanguinary savages," who revered Johnny as a great medicine man, on account of his strange appearance, eccentric actions, and power for enduring pain. (He'd often thrust needles into his flesh.) He'd quench a fire if swarming mosquitoes were killed by the flames. Whenever Johnny saw an animal abused, he would purchase the beast and gift it to a more humane settler.

For thirty-seven years, Johnny's far-flung planting outpaced the advance of civilization, till towns and churches encroached the wilderness, as the stage-driver's horn broke the silence of the grand old woodlands. And so this ragged, homeless benefactor declared his work was done. His labors had borne fruit over a hundred thousand square miles of territory.

"In the summer of 1837," waxed D'Arcy, "with parting words of admonition, Johnny Leviticus Appleseed turned his steps steadily toward the setting sun, unaware that his greatest adventure lay directly before him."

•••••

Following an open-air bivouac, Johnny picked up an old Shawnee trail that felt vaguely familiar. Presently, he broke into meadow he had seeded three decades before—and glared in shock and rage. Ninety acres, where once the seeds of his own planting had blossomed into fruit-bearing trees, were now a wasteland of stumps, the wood hauled off to market. Johnny rent his graying beard, limbs trembling as his spirit boiled over.

He jogged to the nearest settlement and learned that Blue Sky Logging had committed to turning the very forest into a cash crop. The lowest-hanging fruit was Johnny's orchards, full of pernicious crabapples. Though pleasing to the eye, Johnny's fruit made settlers hurl, and gave horses the ague. Indians dried the apples, away from man and beast, and used the withered remnants for their wampum. But applewood remained in high demand from meat smokers; so to head their operation, Big Sky recruited legendary woodsman, Paul Bunyan, who invented the whetstone and logging too. The rapacious axe man who, despite his great size, was so skilled at running over floating timber he could spin the bark off a log and run ashore on the bubbles. Who ran three ten-hour shifts a day and installed the Aurora Borealis, but abandoned the plan because the lights were unreliable.

Paul's partner, Babe the Blue Ox, was forty-two axe handles wide, a bovine locomotive who could pull anything that had two ends to it. Could pull the kinks out of crooked logging roads, even. For a snack between meals, Babe ate fifty bales of hay, bailing wire and all. No orchard, Johnny knew, was safe from Paul Bunyan and his blue ox.

Johnny Appleseed stormed to a clearing, stamped his bare feet, and juddered in deific possession—and received his final mission: stop Paul Bunyan, so help him God.

The first snows had fallen when Johnny tracked down Paul Bunyan at a camp on the fringe of the Appalachias. Johnny's quest for justice was done to death by what he found there.

Babe the Blue Ox had a mania for pancakes and one cooking crew of three hundred men kept busy fashioning cakes for her. Early that morning, Babe had broke from her tether, bull-rushed the cook shanty, and began bolting flapjacks, swallowing the red-hot stove in the process. Indigestion set in and nothing could save her.

Johnny found Paul Bunyan seated in the mud aside his faithful partner. Paul and Johnny recognized each other straightaway, and Paul watched silently as the celebrated planter ran his hand over Babe's cerulean coat. Johnny, apostle of all living things, accepted on the spot his sudden change of fate.

"What do you reckon to do with her, Paul?" asked Johnny.

"Need to get her back to the Dakotas," said Paul. "To bury her proper."

"We'll need a sled."

"I'll fetch the wood."

It took the men a week to build the sled, and another two to convey the Babe three states over to South Dakota, the sled's torturous passage aided by icy terrain. Freezing temperatures preserved the Babe's body, but the brute labor of the haul and the fury of winter drained their life away. Twenty days it took to dig Babe's grave in the flinty terrain, their last and greatest feat.

When they shoveled back the earth, the mound formed its own range, upon which Paul and Johnny laid their bodies to rest, ringed by their beloved wilderness. The snow settled over them, firm as bark. By summer, they mingled with soil and water that drained into rivers and out to the ocean, which would carry the three to the four corners. Their journey would outlive all settlers and no ashes could be strewn more thoroughly—and no monument exist more lasting—than the Black Hills of South Dakota.

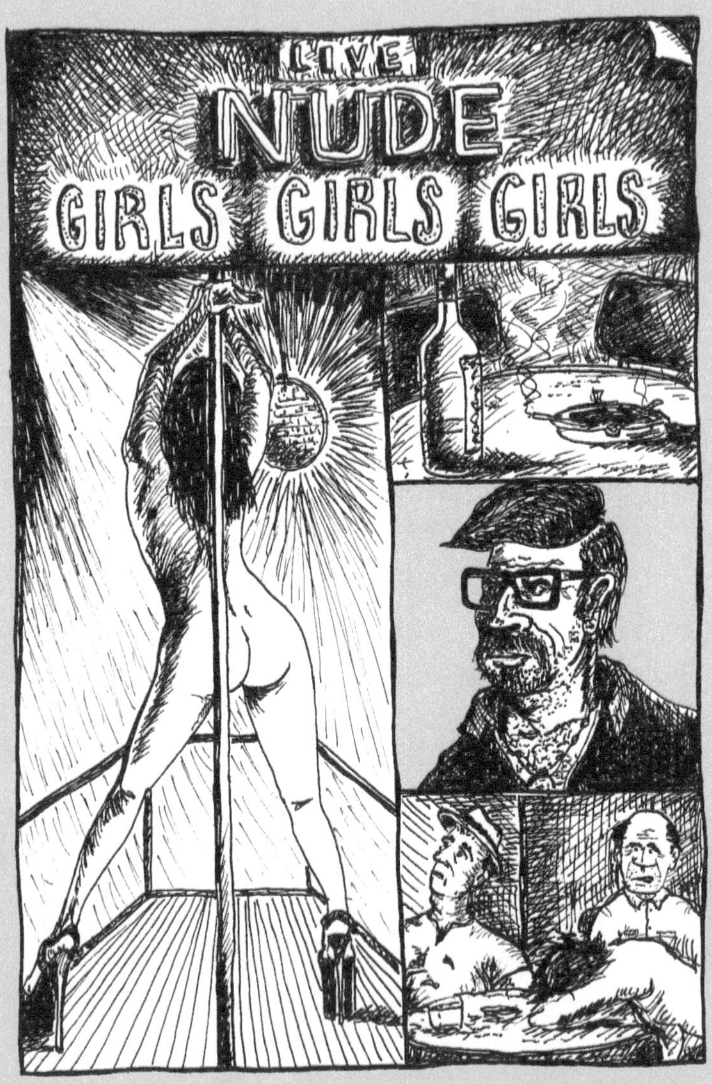
LIVE
NUDE
GIRLS GIRLS GIRLS

LOVE ME TENDER

An editor at Rizzoli sent me the digital galleys for a project called *Glam Utopia* (working title), with stories from Goth girls, call girls, pornstars, and fetish queens, many spangled with colorful tats, and so many piercings you'd swear they fell face-first into a tackle box.

The stories were mostly old news, full of illicit wisdom. But not the last, a shaggy, chaotically unorthodox opus called "Love Me Tender," by Florence Dubois, which had to be her stripper name. The first few graphs ran down Florence's life as an anxious foundling, and how she escaped into books. Then this:

> *Would you tell me, please, which way I ought to go from here?*
> And the Cat said, *That depends a good deal on where you want to get to.*
> *I don't much care where,* I said.
> *Then it doesn't much matter which way you go,* said the Cat.

So long as I get somewhere, I said.

Oh, you're sure to do that, said the Cat, *if only you keep walking.*

So I walked into the seediest strip club in America, and asked the Old Fart for a job.

Picture a one-room dungeon, with plastic chairs arranged around plastic tables, a hole-in-the-wall bar and a T-shaped plywood stage, raised three feet off the ground, with rope lighting and frosted plastic flooring—swank merchandise during the Korean War—plus a tarnished brass railing to prevent the drunken coke whores dancing up there from toppling overboard. The walls are covered with fake rosewood paneling and the China Town décor that hasn't changed since the Clinton Administration.

The owner is seventy-two years young, a perpetually pissy, toxically sentimental Old Fart with an amazing toupee and fancy black-framed glasses, who also doubles as DJ. That means handing him my CDs and praying he remembers the track numbers, lest he gets roaring mad and plays Lords of Acid, whereby I jiggle my cargo on stage to the raunchy strains of "Lick my Chakra" or "Doggy Tom." There are no bouncers or doormen, as the Old Fart, frugal as Scrooge, has claimed both jobs for himself.

Of course, every strip club is a carnival. So are *Vogue* fashion shoots, the *Sports Illustrated* swimsuit issue, the haute couture runway, and a porno shoot in Chatsworth, California. They're all rings of the flesh trade, and everyone working the show is a carny. The runway crowd dresses fancy and tends toward lattes and Pinot Noirs, so forget the Schlitz Malt; but they're carnies just the same, including the clod with the ascot and the silly red glasses. Every carny has a role, and every carnival has an Old Fart,

> a kind of sleazy Mr. Chips, who tames lions and divas by way of the discipline they secretly desire, and who hoses the shit out of the stalls and sucks money from men and corporations and is a lost soul out beyond the big top. His redemption is back through the desert of his past where he wanders alone, belonging to no one, including himself, which makes him cheap and waspish, for his soul has filled with gravel. He gets weepy over stray dogs and whores with black eyes, so you wonder.
>
> He'll die all by himself with an ashtray full of cigar butts, Nickelodeon blaring on the old TV, and something you couldn't have guessed in a hundred years—like a Purple Heart or a niece with Down syndrome—crying at his feet. Treacle, but true. No one will visit his grave because the show must go on and they already have another DJ and a real bouncer this time. The Old Fart is dead as the eyes of the truckers and roofers and plastic surgeons arrayed around the stage. You lose your fear of death in a carnival, in a strip club, by playing dead yourself. Dope and whisky might help in that regard.

It rambled on for three more pages, in her angel dust rendering of New Journalism. God knows how much of it was true. The actual ending, like a frayed silk stocking, ran like this:

> I grew up in a madhouse, with no meaning, no unity, truth, or values, and no God but a zealot with a bag full of snakes. Life is heinous, but I don't need to kill myself. I need to revolt. And I did, when I fled the dungeon for good. But my feet are heavy, and I tire, ghosted and gaslighted by my truth.
>
> So I told the Cat, *I always walk with my head downward.*
>
> *The antiphonies,* said the Cat. *You left yourself on that plywood stage. We must go back and fetch her.*

But I don't want to go among mad people, I said.

Oh, you can't help that, said the Cat, waving its right paw round.

Then I'm holding onto your tail, I said.

And the Cat said, *That's what it's for.*

MAGNIFICENT LUNKERS AND A BLUE RABBIT'S FOOT

A flock of gulls flapped above the whitecaps on our starboard side.

"Those birds is where the lunkers are," said a nearby angler, who'd just stepped off a logging truck. "We're golden."

I was one of about fifty of us who, early that morning, had stumbled abord the *The Aguaholic,* a clunky old sportfishing trawler with a fifty-four gallon hogshead full of Old Milwaukee beer. "Deep sea drinking." That's how my boss described this half-day junket, which I won in an office raffle.

The anchor dropped, the gulls scattered, and all hands scrambled, snatching up fishing rods as soldiers take up arms, baiting hooks with bloody chunks of eel and ballyhoo. Poles bent, reels sang as whooping anglers reeled in skipjacks, halibut, a spectacular blue marlin, yellowtail, rock cod, and a flounder the size of a collie. All I managed were two stinky little mackerels.

Then something so violently struck my line it nearly jerked me out of my sneakers.

"He's hooked the kraken!" yelled a woman with a Dodgers cap.

When the monster let off for a second, I spooled in some line, as instructed. I didn't know sportfishing from Sacramento.

"Don't lose him, slick!"

Anglers piled against the gunwale, staring below. I widened my stance, cranking on that reel like I meant it. Then got yanked to the edge and nearly overboard. I peered down and saw my hook snagged on a teased-up peroxide mop, rising off the sea as I spooled in line, taut as a bowstring. Then shoulders, a chest.

"*Mr. President*!" someone yelled, as I wound in the former President of the United States of America, Donald John Trump, stuffed into a sharkskin suit.

Twenty paws hauled Mr. President aboard. A deckhand with a vulture tattoo raced over with Vise-Grips and torqued the hook off Mr. President's bouffant, actually your standard comb-over, secured with such gels and lacquers you couldn't have pried it off his skull with Archimedes' lever.

"He hooked the freaking President on a baited line," said a bearded angler in a UC Berkeley sweatshirt.

"Not even," said Vulture, snapping the Vise-Grips in Berkeley's face. "Mr. President don't eat no ballyhoo."

"Not when he can stuff his piehole with Quarter Pounders and Kentucky Fried," laughed the Dodger fan.

"What's wrong with Kentucky Fried?" asked Mr. President, cinching the knot on his tie.

Dodger Fan, confused by an honest question from her sworn enemy, said, "Well, it tastes okay, I guess. But all that grease and sodium . . ."

"You're probably right," said Mr. President. "But they're saying a dash of apple cider vinegar, and a tablespoon of Gunk—"

"The engine degreaser?" several asked in unison.

"My keys," said Mr. President, suddenly remembering. "I'm looking for my keys."

After a puzzling pause, I asked, "What do they look like, Mr. President?"

"They're on a simple ring, with a blue rabbit's foot."

Always a hassle when you lose your keys, but nobody on board had seen them. Vulture checked the poop deck, just to be sure, shaking his head. No keys.

Mr. President shrugged and said, "Well, I'm having such an adventure trying to find them, it's probably just as well." But he didn't sound so sure, looking anxious where the tides were taking him.

"You must have seen some wonders down below," said the Dodger fan, who wanted to believe in rabbits' feet.

Mr. President gazed off in a direction he'd never looked before.

"I've seen sea dragons dancing off the coast of Zanzibar. Humpbacks sucked up the bore of a waterspout. And the mighty blue marlin, Ferrari of the Deep."

"I got your blue marlin right here, Mr. President," said the angler who caught it, proud as the sky. We moved as one, over to the opalescent creature with the polka-dotted sail soaring off its back, the javelin snout, and the scythe-shaped tail, still twitching.

"Magnificent creature," said Mr. President. He slowly drew his fingers along the cerulean, black, bronze, and mother of pearl racing stripes running along the sides of the great fish.

"Pity to leave it here," he said softly, "since nobody ever eats blue marlin."

The angler looked longingly at his catch, the best of his life, and said, "Maybe we should put it back where it belongs."

"That's mighty white . . . err, gracious of you," said Mr. President.

The tides shifted, running in a new heading, rocking *The Aguaholic.*

The moment we settled, six of us gathered up the blue marlin and walked it over to the swinging door on the gunwale, where Mr. President stood, his back to the ocean, both arms outstretched like the statue of *Cristo Redentor*, peering down on Rio from Mount Corcovado.

We set the great fish into the arms of Mr. President, who turned, stepped out into the void, and knifed back into the sea.

L8R XX

COLOR ME GONE

Shadows stole across the desert as we trudged from Ice Box Canyon to the Willow Springs parking area. Wilbur's Mercedes wouldn't start. Lucky for us, a dozen wise guys, all in their late twenties and early thirties, met out there Thursday evenings, to tie one on and bullshit.

Godzilla might have stumbled up, how the wise guys hooted and circled round the moment they spotted Wilbur. I'd grown up with these guys, all sons of old-school gangsters who once ran the Vegas casinos. Wilbur wasn't one of them. Wilbur was a hustler. Wilbur was not his real name. Nothing about a hustler is strictly true or false. We needed a ride back to town. That was true.

Anthony, a generational talent who belonged in a general's uniform, or the governor's office, glowered at Wilbur like he'd scammed his girlfriend. Or all his money. "What's your play here, Wilbur?"

"Just hiking with my bud here."

The others jeered. If they had to know, said Wilbur, he'd hired me to guide him through the Red Rocks, every Thursday, searching for the lost Mormon treasure, stashed in some canyon back in 1848. All of us Vegas kids had heard that silly folktale, and nobody sober ever bought it.

The wise guys looked at me and I said, "He actually believes that shit."

"Maybe," said Anthony. "But the last thing he wants to do is ever find it." He looked at Wilbur. "Call an Uber."

"They can't make pick-ups in state parks," said Wilbur.

"Looks like you're hoofin' it, then," said Dino.

They laughed again. But ditching Wilbur meant missing the chance to try and bust his "gaff," or swindle, which damn straight was on because Wilbur kept acting like it wasn't. He'd pulled fast ones on these guys since junior high. Had hustled them at golf, billiards, poker—anything wise guys bet on. And they bet on everything because life only ignited when they had skin in the game. So six of us slid into Anthony's vintage Cadillac El Dorado and he gunned it for Las Vegas, thirty empty miles due east.

Didn't Wilbur owe Mr. V. a grand from the Super Bowl? Nick wanted to know.

No, he didn't.

How come Wilbur only gave Rudy the heads-up about the Raiders game?

Rudy should have told the others. Blame him.

How about Wilbur touching old man Ricci for fifteen K on the Lopez fight?

"Lucky you're still breathing," said Dino, riding shotgun.

Anthony kept eying Wilbur in the rearview mirror, and the whoppers kept coming. Wilbur winning The Reno Bowling Tourney with a doctored ball. Wilbur tipping them off about the

Preakness, only to have Wilbur fleece their winnings the next week, playing Texas hold 'em at Binion's.

Anthony hooked a left off the Red Rock loop road onto the 159, just missing a speeding Rolling Rock beer truck, and headed for town. Just right lay a huge, light-skinned dog sprawled out on the shoulder. Roadkill.

"Christ," said Nick, sitting in back with us. "You run a cur down like that, drag the bastard off the highway anyway."

"Better get those eyes checked, Nick," said Wilbur. "Wasn't a dog."

"Hell it wasn't," said Sal, who'd bathed in Old Spice. "Couldn't tell you what kind, though."

"That there," said Wilbur, "was a White Yorkshire pig. From the swine farm down in Blue Diamond."

We all bust out laughing. Wilbur didn't relent. It was a pig back there. "Let it be true," he said, "because it is."

The gaff was officially *on*. I knew it, God knew it, everyone in that Caddy knew it. And we all believed that this time, we had the winning hand—which is why Vegas shines like it does, and Wilbur drove an S-Class Mercedes. For a breathless moment, you could hear molecules colliding in mid-air—till Matteo finally said it: "You wanna bet?"

"Only want a ride back to town," said Wilbur.

"Hear that?" said Nick. "Wilbur won't take your stakes."

"I don't wanna take your damn money," said Wilbur. "All you mugs are sore losers."

Anthony pulled over and got out. The rest of us followed, all eyes looking back toward the dead dog, maybe a quarter mile behind us. Not a car on the road. Nothing but gray desert sand, flat as a snooker table, stretching several miles out to the deep canyons and soaring buttes of the Red Rocks. If so much as a jackrabbit had moved on this empty plane, we would have seen it.

"Imagine that," said Anthony. "Wilbur passing on a bet?"

"I have to be at Caesars by nine," said Wilbur. "And I'm not holding much, besides."

"You're good for it," said Nic.

"Or we carve it outta you later, if you ain't," said Dino.

Anthony smiled wryly at Wilbur. Back in grade school, they'd both been in the GATE (Gifted and Talented Education) program, while the rest of us were pestering girls and choking on Marlboros behind the maintenance shed. If they hadn't helped us with our homework—or just did it for us—we all would have failed. The business here was between Anthony and Wilbur. The rest of us were playing in a minor key, like we always had around these two *pezzo da novantas*.

"You're taking the bet, Wilbur," said Anthony. "Or you're walking to Caesars. But no funny business."

Wilbur laughed, swished his hands at the empty desert, and said, "Like how?"

They all howled. Wilbur was funny business. But unless Wilbur could turn a dog into a pig, from distance, this time, at long last, the wise guys had him by the short hairs.

"We better walk," I said.

"Stay outta this," said Matteo.

The four wise guys, who always carried wads of cash, had a little over eleven grand between them. Anthony gathered the bankroll, handed it to me and said, "Hold that."

"You hold it," I said.

"Don't worry, slick," said Anthony. "You'll be handing it over in a minute."

Anthony drove us back to the turnout. We all piled out—and froze.

"That porker ain't what I seen before," growled Nick, eyes fixed on the big pink pig, lying where the dog had been. "I know that for a fact."

"Can't say how you done it, but you swapped 'em," said Dino, getting up in Wilbur's face.

"Like when," said Wilbur. "Or how?" He glanced at me and said, "Give 'em their money back."

I held out the wad to Anthony, who shook his head at the pig and chuckled. These guys would game the Pope at seven card stud, but you don't go squelching on a bet. That's dishonorable.

Dino went over and kicked the pig while Matteo ranged around, looking for a hole somebody might have hidden in with a giant dead hog. But there was nothing but gray sand and tumbleweeds for as far as the eye could see.

Anthony looked expansive as the desert. Whenever he and Wilbur crossed paths, they saw in the other the mole hill where they'd both ended up. But this encounter had a greatness to it.

"Cheer up, *guidos*," said Anthony. "They'll be talking about this grift for a hundred years . . . and we'll always be a part of it." He nodded at Wilbur and said, "Color me gone. But you're walking, Wilbur." And he left us on the road with all their money.

"I let you in on this beforehand," said Wilbur, "your nerves would'a tipped them off. This oughta cover it."

Wilbur peeled five hundred-dollar bills off the bank roll and handed them to me.

"Don't try that again," I said, taking the money.

Half an hour later, the Rolling Rock beer truck looped back and snagged us. A giant, stuffed, polyester Mastiff, bought from the retail shop at Circus Circus Casino, lay sprawled out in back. Wilbur handed $1,200 to the driver.

"Glad we made some run-throughs," said the driver. "I barely made the swap and got outta range when Tony headed back."

The seventeen hundred to the driver and me, plus the seven bills he paid for the hog, left Wilbur with around nine grand, most of which he'd conveniently lose back to the wise guys. This balanced the books, between grudging childhood friends, and opened the door for Wilbur's next play, which made their world go round. Neither Wilbur nor Anthony much cared about the money. But a top-shelf gaff gave both momentary shelter from the regrets that pooled in the hearts of every clever wise guy and hustler I'd ever known.

VANISHING POINT

I knew by heart her faint *knock knock knock*. Fair warning that the door would ease open and she'd be standing there, lighting up the doorway, one foot drumming the floor. I had seconds to shove everything aside and rollerblade down to Redondo Beach, or mountain bike to Utah, with Dacia, the nutritionist at Gold's Gym Venice. She'd gotten bored (always a five-alarm crisis) and had to do something hard, preferably risky, to "extirpate the funk" (her term—she read books). Half the time, I was banging on *her* door, needing to get moving, faster the better, or implode. I hadn't yet learned how to drink.

This time, I hardly recognized Dacia, leaning against my doorjamb, her mouth thrown open, breathing in reeling gasps. She'd gotten to my place so quickly she must have texted me from out front. We always rushed to each other when the way ahead dead-ended.

I steered her onto my couch. She slumped and shook, rocking

back and forth. Like someone clutched in that clammy fugue state you get from eating bad oysters, before you heave your guts out. Made me feel like a heel for wanting to rip her clothes off the first 500 times we did stuff. "Save it for when I need you," she laughed. Someday, like now, she'd call it in. I hadn't a clue.

Tortured animal sounds rushed out of her, shrieks and wails that went beyond pain in every direction. Then crying for real. I'd never been this close to such grief.

Our friend Shelly called the week before, saying Dacia's baby was born with a bad heart and died after two days. Dacia's parents lived in Laguna Beach, forty-five minutes south, so she must have followed them back to California after the services in Colorado. I never ever expected her to show up at my place so soon. I got her a glass of water, and she started blaming herself. Little splinters of guilty thoughts. Each one said more to herself than to me.

She knew damn well she was blowing out her system, competing in all those adventure races (she repeatedly won the Raid Gallouis and Eco Challenge), where she'd sometimes charge for ten days with almost no sleep. She'd return home with separated shoulders, torn ACLs, twice with giardia. She'd barely move for weeks and didn't have her period for months. Not till she turned forty-two did she get married and try and have kids, ignoring doctor's warnings she was high risk. She'd hardly given her baby a chance. That's how Dacia saw it, anyway.

"I never got to hold her," she said, with the lifeless eyes of a mother still peering through the window of the ICU.

A live birth meant a birth certificate, a given name, a death certificate, she said in fits and starts. And burying a little coffin in Crested Butte, all quaking aspens and icy peaks, where she lived with her new husband.

"How do I do this?" she asked, her eyes so red and swollen she could barely keep them open.

“I think you’re doing it,” I said. “But I couldn’t tell you how.”

She toyed with my bike helmet, lying next to her on the couch, and said, “The next ten feet.” A little air rushed into the room.

We could never, in one go, pedal up Mt. Washington, climb Half Dome, or paddle the Bio Bio. But we could usually manage the next ten feet. Then the next ten. All the way to the vanishing point.

THE LEGEND OF HURACÁN HERNÁNDEZ

From his first matches in La Arena México, to his ascension as a national icon, Huracán Hernández pulled *lucha libre* off the wrestling mat and hurled it into mid-air. And he took all of us right along with him.

Who would ever have imagined a *luchador* throwing a double gainer off the top of the ring post, and landing with his legs scissored around the neck of Terrible Teodoro, the giant who crushed golf balls in his bare hands and ripped the mask off El Loco? Yet for all of his high flying acrobatics, Huracán's renown rests largely on how he addressed the burning question per all heroes, clowns, and villains of the prize ring: who was that man behind the mask?

Tradition dictates all wrestlers sport sparkly colored masks, enriched with kitschy embroidery. Huracán's initial facade—which encircled his entire *cabeza*—was jet black muslin, with pin holes for his eyes, and a thin silver zipper sewn across his mouth. A disguise "cobbled from a dominatrix's livery and Dracula's old napkins," as sportswriter Geronimo Suárez once wrote. An odd but fitting mask for a *Rudo* like Huracán, monarch of urban masculinity, in his pitched battles against the handsome and heroic Técnicos, who follows all the rules.

The legend of Huracán Hernández, and the social reform he spawned, corresponds to both the progressive transparency of his masks and his full disclosure as a person. An existential salvage job experienced by an entire people, which gave street urchins and presidents, and all of us in between, a shooting star to wish upon.

The first phase of the Huracán Miracle finds the *luchador* donning his jet black mask both in the ring and in public at large, including Sunday mass. No celebrity in memory so doggedly guarded his private life (his true identity was known only to his agent, Don Plutarco Delgado-Figueroa). For most of those early years, Huracán Hernández remained the most mysterious *hombre* in Latin America.

Columnist Federico Morales, during a tournament in Chihuahua, first noticed the change in Huracán's mask—from solid black muslin to a woven black cotton. He'd also widened the eye holes and cut a small breach for his mouth. This begat the *luchador* a more human aspect, as opposed to the menacing black bug look of his breakout campaigns. We also witnessed the first confessions about his private identity, on TV and radio talk shows, where Huracán courageously owned his hardscrabble youth.

Over the following dozen years, as Huracán thrust his high-flying act into the troposphere, his masks grew so scant that during his final bout at El Palacio, Estado Durango, his face was covered by little more than a black fishnet. Meanwhile we learned how Huracán had once been a Mexican Artful Dodger, who grew up *peso*less on the streets of Tepito, picking pockets and stealing food. He didn't know a single relative, and had no documents proving that he'd ever been born. "That's who I am," he said.

Nothing short of full transparency could have better humanized the champion, or kick-started social justice programs from Tijuana to Tierra del Fuego. But Huracán's greatest triumph, according to Padre Juan Miguel Bustos (Archbishop of Tampico, and advisor to the *luchador*), was "confirming for all the dignity of the human soul." It was only fitting that we observed a national day of mourning when, last week, pancreatic cancer carried Huracán Hernández away from us.

The memorial, held at La Basílica de Nuestra Señora de Guadalupe, saw an estimated quarter million fans pay homage to Huracán Hernández, at rest in his open casket. Many were nonplussed that undertakers had fitted the wrestler with his old black muslin mask. Was that actually Señor Huracán, lying silent in the gold *ataúd*? No one could tell with that mask pulled over his face. And for a hero who confirmed the promise of *todos humanos*, why not lose the mask altogether, for his final act on this earth? Journalist Teressa Blanco, at *El Diario*, put the question to Huracán's longtime agent, Don Plutarco Delgado-Figueroa.

"Huracán Hernández first entered the prize ring with a great fear," said Don Plutarco. "A fear that he should be found out as a peon, and shunned. A fear Huracán never entirely escaped. So now, traveling to a new arena, with an all-powerful referee, Huracán chose to once again debut incognito. To get a feel for the heavenly *torneo*, the size and sentiment of the crowd, that he might better come to know, and meet, their needs. Of course, such things take time. And maybe the angels and saints are bored, because in heaven, all the interesting people are missing."

The old agent, on whose sofa Huracán Hernández once slept, cracked a knowing grin.

"But the moment they see Huracán," said Don Plutarco, "throwing his *Sacacorchos 450 Splash*, his *Lariat de Pierna Giratoria*, and his *Plancha de Salto Mortal de Paseo por la Cuerda. Caramba!* Just watch them throw their harps and jump off their thrones and welcome Huracán Hernández to the Promised Land."

And then, just maybe, Huracán Hernández might finally take off his mask, and be among his people.

BONE ON BONE

I rarely thought about drinking anymore, but a few times a week, I still went to an evening meeting down on 3rd and Wilshire. And Gina A. walks in. Like a poem strolling into a locker room. She'd gotten a DUI and the court sent her there. The woman sitting beside her, in fashionably ripped jeans and hog boots, had to be her sponsor.

Once the meeting opened up for sharing, hog boots gently nudged Gina. Twice. She had to share. All eyes were on her when she did.

"I'm Gina and I'm not some rummy," she assured us. "But I made a mistake and, actually, it's interesting to hear all your stories." Yada yada. Newcomers often talk sideways like that. A feeling of pantomime attaching to their words, as if they were trying on the program for a lark.

Over the following few weeks, Gina kept showing up in sleeveless wrap dresses, her hair French-braided just so, or swept into a chignon. But something felt secondhand about her whole display, as if she'd copied it straight off some diva's mood board. When I shared about tensions with my girlfriend, because I wouldn't move to Switzerland, Gina grabbed me after the meeting and said she'd only recently moved back from Geneva. She'd heard I climbed some and I had to take her. She'd climbed "a ton."

Week after week, Gina kept hounding me to take her climbing and I kept making excuses. The woman felt sketchy, someone God never intended. But I was an alcoholic, with a weakness for misfits and, most of all, trouble. So one evening, I met Gina at Rocreation, a local climbing gym. It didn't end well.

Year and a half later, I'm hobbling down the darkened aisle of Swiss Air flight 445 to Zurich when I see, of all the people in all the world, Gina-Fucking-A., with a fleece blanket laying across her lap. Sitting between two middle-aged men in casual business clothes. The guy sitting in the aisle seat offered her an open bottle of water. She shook her head, looking straight ahead with a baleful scowl. I swept past her unnoticed, reminded of the woman with every step, when my ankle ground bone on bone.

The flight attendants had gone into hiding as the passengers dozed, but a big lighted space in the rear of the airbus overflowed with beverages and snacks any passenger could pillage at leisure. I stewed back there for an age, scarfing chocolates, wondering what atrocity I might commit on Gina and not do time—till the man sitting in the aisle seat next to her wandered back for a coffee. He knew her for sure, the way he offered her water like that, and how she busted his balls with that arctic look.

"That woman you're sitting next to," I said. "Gina A." That got his attention. "There's something you should know about her."

"Go on," he said in accented English, topping off his coffee.

I skipped the AA backstory and went straight to meeting Gina at the climbing gym. She moved well and knew the ropes. Not a beginner. I belayed her up several routes, then I took a burn up an easy climb. The second I reached the anchor on top and leaned back to get lowered off, she simply let go of the rope, which you never do since there's nothing holding the climber's weight for the lower-off. I free-fell twenty-five feet straight into the deck, landing on my feet.

The first thing I saw when I rolled up was my tibia jutting from a fist-sized hole in my shin. While the staff freaked out and paramedics rushed in, Gina slipped out of the gym unnoticed. I spent the next forty days at Cedars-Sinai Medical Center as orthopedists screwed my leg back together and plastic surgeons harvested a muscle off my thigh and stitched it into the crater in my shin. Never heard a word from Gina. She dropped me like a rock, and vanished. Whole thing cost over four hundred grand. I was on the hook for 45K of it, and was still paying that off.

The guy took a last sip of coffee and said, "Sorry about the leg. That's—how do you say—harsh." He tossed his cup in the trash. "I am not her boyfriend, if that is what you think."

"Not your fault if you are."

He glanced down the aisle and opened his wallet, showing his Swiss INTERPOL badge with the red-and-white cross. I stared at the shiny badge for a second, till I got it.

"That blanket on her lap is hiding the handcuffs."

He nodded. "We extradite her, back to Geneva. The guy sitting next, in the window seat, is a US Air Marshall. Just to make sure."

"What's the charge?"

He smiled and raised a hand. He couldn't say.

I gave the guy a minute to go back and get situated, and started walking back to my seat. I wanted to stop, grab Gina by an ear, and give her forty-five grand worth of grief. There was no satisfaction in having the Swiss do it for me. But the eye of the needle was straight ahead, so I kept hobbling away, bone on bone.

E R

NO TIME TO DIE

He donned his white tuxedo, drove the Aston Martin to the Casino de Monte-Carlo, took his seat at the baccarat table, and pulled winner after winner from the shoe.

The countess fancied his saucy patter. And his wink when he dealt her a natural nine. Glorious were the champagne and beluga caviar he ordered up to the penthouse. More so the naughty nothings, coyly whispered. Skin to skin. Her arching sigh. Then the tragic humiliation when James Bond could not draw solid wood. Next night, with the Nigerian diplomat, and the following evening, with the Korean physicist—same deal.

James Bond cringed to think how Moneypenny, and all the others, would respond to his double entendres, once they discovered his empty gun. James Bond would strangle any doctor who uttered the words *erectile dysfunction*, because he was James-Fucking-Bond, who crammed his fridge, and his person, with libido enhancers: bars of Swiss chocolate, mouth-blistering peppers. He couldn't scrub the stink of blowfish off his plimsolls, and if he ate another pipe of asparagus, he'd turn green. Some rhino horn was on the way, but as it stood, or didn't, the timber would not rise.

James Bond sealed the blinds, seized a bottle of Beefeater Dry, and chunked down onto his sofa. Last time he touched bottom like this, Vesper Lynd loved him past the gunplay and rakery and back to humanity. If only by a crosshair. But Vesper drowned, and now with the poplar at parade rest, James Bond found himself in freefall.

He pitchpoled back, crash landing in a tiny room in the rural flat of his paternal aunt, shortly after his parents died in a mountaineering accident near Chamonix. James Bond, then eleven years old, felt gutted as a Tom Turkey. Young James never thought about God, but he sent up a prayer, just hoping that he might become someone valiant and essential enough to fill the void inside him. With nothing more to lose, he took liberties others would never consider, and saved the world a dozen times. Now there were calls to cancel 007, a cartoonish cipher of a man in designer kit who, if the mood took him, could kill or shag anyone in the room. Commander James Herbert Bond was a relic.

"Says who?" James Bond snarled. Just a clutch of thankless fops, taking their vegan biscuits at the club while deconstructing Plath and raving on social media. Somebody had to wrangle the Hugo Draxes and Ernst Blofelds. And you don't lay woke blather on Oddjob. You shoot him dead, or there is no club. And if James Bond was the avatar for White Knight Hero Syndrome, how was that his fault?

But where did it leave him now?

James Bond studied the Beefeater bottle, where smack dab in the middle stood a tony Yeoman Warden in a red dress uniform, guarding the Tower of London, as they have since Tudor times. James felt a stiffening he tried to ignore. But he could no longer conceal, especially from himself, his passion for men in scarlet pantaloons. For men in hand-tooled boots and big black cowboy hats. For men! James Bond loved him some women, but he'd overplayed his hand to try and deny the undeniable: 007 was a natural-born switch-hitter, who kept eyeing the Yeoman Warden as the timber soared, indominable as Big Ben. And bugger the bloody blowfish.

As night slid into dawn, James Bond slowly settled, like bitters in a martini. His ability to do so in crisis had averted global destruction, a nuclear holocaust, World War III. The list was Homeric. But could he surf past the white knight fable and vanquish the void inside him? Only if he outed the true James Bond to the Home Office, to his many colleagues, friends and foes, and to the world. Delicate work that could backfire horribly. No guarantees either way, but there never had been—not with Dr. Julius No or Rosa Klebb, Francisco Scaramanga or all the rest. James Bond killed the Beefeater and cracked a cheeky smile.

"I'll figure this out," he said, jumping into his shooting stance, clicking his heels for good measure. "I'm still James-Fucking-Bond."

ICE

I started pulling the rappel ropes, doubled through the anchor up above, when the free end got stuck in the crack.

"Shit!" Ed yelled. "We're toast . . ."

Warming days (which melted the high-country snowpack) and freezing nights had rimmed El Capitan with ice. Small beer when gazing from the Loop Road, a mile away and 3,000 feet below the rim. But scope it through binos and you'll see an ice crown forty feet tall and just as thick, with hundred-foot icicles dangling below. Once sunlight hits the crown, chunks calve off and torpedo the lower slabs. The sun was already wrapping around the East Buttress. We had to get off this thing. Like now.

By the time we freed the rope, the ice crown gleamed like a mirror. Huge drops, impossibly cold, pocked the face left and right. Ed shot down the last rappel at 20 MPH, touching ground as the first icy missiles dashed the face.

"Go! *GO!*" I yelled, but didn't need to.

Ed shot off and down the bushy moraine field, hopping block to block. Slaloming around bushes and towering pines. Then gone.

Lashed to two bolts, I was a hanging duck. I hurried to thread the rope through my rappel device—then the *CRACK*, thousands of feet above.

A glimmering mass the size of a school bus slowly rotated in midair, freefalling straight for me. I pill-bugged as the chunk fell half a mile, which must have taken ten seconds. An eternity. And the whole time I'm cursing myself for losing my girlfriend's keys the previous night, both of us searching for hours, chastising the other for losing them. And how things heated up early that morning and I got pissed off and bolted up here at 6:30 a.m. with Ed.

The giant chunk of ice detonated on the slabs above.

Huge ice bollards shrieked past like meteors, exploding off the rock. Crashing off the talus at the base. Shrapnel caroming 100 feet into the moraine field and blowing limbs off trees. That I wasn't smeared off my belay anchor was the dumbest luck.

I rappelled to the ground in seconds flat as another barrage carpet-bombed the talus. I dove under a little overhang—a granite awning to deflect direct strikes—but ricocheting shards stung like buckshot, and I bled from a thousand little cuts.

Just as I'm fixing to dash for it, a big *thump* sounds from the slabs above. Followed by shrill whirring, like the antiaircraft missiles I've seen in war docs. Not fifty feet away, right at the edge of the trees, a five-story, diamond-hard icicle augured straight into the deck, dematerializing into an exploding mushroom cloud of shards and cubes, as the end chased after, consuming the point. Then—nothing but splattering drops.

I hand-checked myself. Nothing mashed or missing. My heart banged away but my mind felt clear, and I *saw* where I'd put the goddam ring of keys last night. I didn't appreciate my altered state, that a shockwave had blown me back a day, and I remembered the last thing I'd forgotten—till Ed shouted up from the tree line.

For a moment, I sat as frozen as the ice crown. Then jerked, as if electrocuted, jumping to my feet.

"Still here!" I yelled back.

"Run for it, dumbass!" Ed yelled.

That's why they call them "partners."

I dashed after Ed, taking cover behind the downhill side of big Jeffery pines as grenades exploded all around. Finally, we cleared the impact zone.

On the Loop Road at last, I drove straight to Sherri's cabin and pulled the big ring of keys from the trunk lock in her rusty Dodge Dart. She met me at the door.

"My bad," I said, holding up the ring. "I left them stuck in your trunk."

She grabbed the ring and held it to her chest. She ran the night desk at Yosemite Lodge, and the ring had her work keys on it.

"Whatever happened to you," she said, frowning at the cuts on my hands and face, "you deserve it." She'd searched all morning for those keys, while I went climbing. A selfish move, and I said so. She finally cracked a little smirk—meaning I was forgiven, again—and said, "You look dehydrated."

She grabbed a plastic bottle of Gatorade from the fridge, then opened the freezer. I grabbed the bottle and pushed the door shut.

"No ice."

ROTTEN LUCK

Hours jouncing over dirt roads, winding through the heart of the Andes, to Casa de Piedra—the Rock House. Then slogging over the sandy plain to Plaza Argentina and Base Camp. Two *burros* carried their food, tents, and several prepared meals. Guides Luis Manual and Roberto began divvying the gear for the steepening march to Plaza Canadá, the first mountain camp at 16,570 feet.

"You might have mentioned the girl tagging along," said Dustin, a strapping Californian. He and the others would have to carry more, which cut their chances of summiting. Always a crap-shoot on these blitz attempts, when you swoop onto the mountain and charge.

"Everyone carries the same load," said Roberto. He had a scale to make sure. Dustin groused and turned away.

Two days later, they trudged into Acampar Berlín, the High Camp. Luis Manuel split the dozen clients into four small teams. They'd rope back up in the wee hours, and quest for the top.

Summit Day meant hours above 20,000 feet, so get good and hydrated, he said. Then try and rest for a few hours.

The group huddled around the stove, talking small and nervously. Drinking as much hot tea as they could stomach. Karin mentioned she had two young boys waiting for her in Portland. Dustin looked alarmed that she ever chose to climb that mountain with children back home.

"Do you have kids?" she asked.

Of course he did. He stripped off his gloves and passed around a wallet photo showing two teenaged girls holding handfuls of stones he had packed off various summits. A reddish rhyolite flake from Chimborazo. A feldspar crystal off Mt. Kenya. Souvenirs for his girls. Now he'd go get them a stone off the top of Aconcagua, the highest mountain in the western hemisphere. Karin studied the photo.

"I'm sure they make you proud," said Karin.

He shot Karin a look and said, "They're very proud of their father. Just a regular guy—with dreams."

The dream died in the wee hours, when Dustin got altitude sickness and Roberto started leading him down to Base Camp. Karin and her teammates wished the two good luck on getting down, and rallied for their summit push. Stopping many times during the following hours. Pushing around the gendarmes and under the summit overhangs to finally top out. Then four exhausting hours stumbling back down to Camp 2, and another day's trudge to lower altitudes, and Base Camp at Plaza Argentina.

Roberto and Dustin met the group a mile up the sandy trail above Base Camp. Dustin, riding a *burro*, appeared in fine spirits. "Nothing but rotten luck," he said. "Altitude sickness can get anyone. I'll return."

Everyone knew Dustin was sounding off, that he and Aconcagua were done with each other.

Karin went over, pressed a little black-flecked stone into Dustin's hand, and said, "Give that to your girls, from me. Girls dream too, you know."

"That's what I'm afraid of," he said, with surprising candor. He wrapped his fingers around the small stone, heavy as Gibraltar in his hand.

“SO I BIT ITS BALLS”

> A Louisiana truck stop turned into a real zoo when a woman (identified as Rhonda Bodine) chomped down on a camel’s testicles while trying to retrieve her dog that had scrambled into the dromedary’s den.

Mercy. Another daft email from my old roommate, Ted, songwriter and “large installation painter” (houses), who’d cut and paste breaking news stories from the tabloids, notorious for boorish headlines like, “Elton Takes David Up The Aisle,” and “Headless Body in Topless Bar.” I read on, like I always did.

> The showdown between Rhonda and Caspar the camel, a roadside attraction, happened Thursday at a truck stop in Gross Tete, about twenty

> minutes outside Baton Rouge. Rhonda's husband began tossing Milk Bones under Caspar's fence, prompting their poodle to wheedle under the barbed wire and into the enclosure, according to Sergeant Lester Bethune of the Iberville Parish Sheriff's Office.
>
> Rhonda Bodine scrambled after Jofi (the dog)—but she didn't get far before Caspar took a seat on top of her. Male dromedaries can weigh up to 1,300 pounds, according to Ambrose Mahoney, Zookeeper at Lion Country Safari in West Palm Beach, FL; meaning the missus was under meaningful pressure to take decisive action.
>
> "So I bit his balls to get him off of me," said Rhonda.

The journalist (or more likely, Ted himself) had evidently doctored the names. Ambrose Mahoney (a made-up moniker for sure), Bodine (cribbed from the old *Beverly Hillbillies* series), and Jofi (Sigmund Freud's dog), signaled corn-pone touches that, when caught by certain readers, make them feel clever. The vanity of rubes. Like Ted. I finished the short read.

> "Casper did nothing wrong," said Sergeant Bethune. "The couple was reckless and aggressive. The humper was just doing its normal routine."
>
> "My only question to her husband was: *Why did you chuck doggy treats under the fencing?*" Bethune recalled. "And he just said, 'I wasn't thinking.'"

> "He's really a gentle giant," Bethune said of Caspar.
>
> The Bodines were cited with a leash law violation for letting the dog run free on private property, as well as criminal trespassing.

Not till finishing the fool article did I remember what Ted wrote in the *Subject* bar of his email: *Don't sit on the Missus Bodine.*

IQ TEST

A Mule is the offspring of a male Donkey and a female Horse.

A Burro is the Spanish name for Mule.

A male Zebra and female Donkey produce a Zonkey (aka, Zebonkey, Zebrinny, and Zebrula).

A male Zebra crossed with a Horse, renders a Zorse, including the Zalimino, Zapalossa, and the Tanzanian Walking Zorse.

A male Zebra and a female Pony give us the Zony.

What's a Zackass?

THE IDIOT

Marta had already served nearly seven years of an eight-year manslaughter rap. Now her last review before the board. If they let her out early, it wouldn't be by much.

"If you have anything to say," said a board woman, "we'd love to hear it—*so long as it's true.*"

"Dostoevsky," said Marta, to no one in particular. "A Russian who wrote a book. About a man who told the truth. All the time. He called it, *The Idiot.*"

The director (there for an HBO series on female inmates) and I stood peering through a one-way mirror and into the small conference room, with a crackly speaker off to our side. Behind the glass, seated in a plastic chair, Marta faced a five-person parole board: three women and two men.

If the board was naïve, she said, it was because they believed the girls who crashed into that place had the faintest idea about the truth. She looked at the five faces in turn. Hesitating. Why bother telling anything to people who'd heard so many lies they likely could believe nothing else. She pushed on, sounding flat as

Lake Eerie at night.

She'd arrived there with a vicious past and no education—but so what. Millions had the same story, or worse. Like all the rest, she had to survive, with the truth as her worst enemy. Her whole life was geared to crush the truth and create something different. "But I had no means to do any such thing."

The woman looked so raw and felt so human that my toes started curling in my shoes as I tried to imagine her shooting someone dead—or whatever had happened. A silver-haired woman with braids and a Navajo shawl asked what she planned to do.

"I got a scholarship to cooking school," said Marta. "Soon as I get out."

The board denied her release. A few months later, testimony in an unrelated trial led to the discovery that Marta had nothing to do with any manslaughter. Marta never argued her case in court or in prison, and I wondered why she feared being innocent—because I never was. I wanted some of hers.

The HBO director later tracked her down to a restaurant in west Chicago, but Marta had little to say. I'd returned for the White Sox Division Championships and found her working as a pastry chef in a lakeside bistro. I took her to the Sox game and we ended up back at her place, a smallish joint but with a nice view overlooking the water.

We talked small for a while, and she drank a little red she had brought home from the bistro. But a ten-ton elephant stood between us. After a glass or two, it started talking.

She had no foundation, no structure, nothing inside her before they locked her up—and not a clue what to do with herself "inside." She always felt scared, she said. Always freaked out. Freefalling—why or through what, she didn't say. Only that in lock-down, she had a roof, a secure place, a routine, and a few teachers who knew something. It took her most of a decade, literally tied to a stake, to learn how to sneak up on freedom.

"I still feel wobbly and scared half the time, but now I see a future," she said. I asked what she did when she got scared, and she played me a song from Zero 7 about catching a falling star.

I couldn't grab at her, pull her down to my level, and still stay sober. So I slept on the couch and got up in the dark because I was off to Orlando on the eight o'clock.

I showered and dressed at the picture window as the blue drench broke over the lake—and all that yawning freedom.

HE QUIT SNORING

a drabble

"Derned if Clem Chickasaw weren't killed last week, sleeping off a drunk at Grass Range. Seems Clem was pretty well lit, but wanted more. So the sumbitch goes and sacks a booze joint. After smoking up the place and running everybody off, he helps himself to the hooch and passes out cold. Folks all the way over in Waco thought they heard a twister building, but it were only Clem sawing his cord of wood. Anyhow, the booze boss goes and gets a gun and comes back and catches Clem slumbering. Old Clem never woke up—but he quit snoring."

—a letter by Judge Roy Cotton to his brother,
Amarillo, Texas, 1873.

THE UNDISCOVERED BAYOU

Gator popped the tab on a Mountain Dew and handed it to Jeb, whose old pickup clattered past corn fields rising on both sides.

"Who names their kid Hamlet?" asked Gator, referring to the cashier at Harlan's Station: Locksmith, Liquor, and Donuts, where they'd just stopped.

"Somebody likes 'em some Shakespeare," said Jeb.

"Billy Shakespeare," said Gator. "Heard about him."

"Prince Hamlet be one of Billy's boys. 'Member the feller noodling that skull?"

"'Course," said Gator. "What fer you reckon he was noodling?"

"We is, or we ain't. That was his question," said Jeb.

Gator chuckled. "If 'ain't' be nothin', there ain't no 'we' that ain't."

"Reckon not," said Jeb. He chewed off half an acre of apple fritter and washed it home with the Dew. "But ol' Hamlet's way north of tall cotton," Jeb went on. "His ma's taken up with his uncle, who murdered his pappy the month before."

"Lickity split, that uncle," said Gator.

"And a chigger on Hamlet's honor," said Jeb. "He's all bass-akwards, not right in the head, squatting on the edge of the castle."

"Needs him some fog, to boot," said Gator. "Ain't a real castle without fog."

"Gots your fog all around," said Jeb. "Big waves is crashing below, and Hamlet's got a big pigsticker in his hands. Sharp as a preacher's pecker."

Gator looked alarmed. "Ol' Hamy's gonna do himself?"

"He's teetering on the brink," said Jeb. "Should he suffer the varmint and mule heads? Or sink the shiv through the whole shebang."

"That be the question," said Gator.

"If he offs his own self, he ain't," said Jeb.

"No whips, no scorn, no sorrows," said Gator.

"Just the big sleep. Maybe some dreamin'."

"That's a farm-sized 'maybe,'" said Gator.

"It's out yonder past figuring."

"So we noodle away, and tucker the yapper—"

"And wonder," said Jeb. "What dreams hound the dead man's doze?"

"If the man upstairs gives life," said Gator, "and we toss it to the worms—"

"Jehovah might get sore," said Jeb. "And nightmares is comin'. And flames, just maybe."

"And judgements, fierce as shine. That's the rub," said Gator, peering past the fields, where a gibbous moon soared off a darkening ridgeline. He snapped a suspender and said, "What is we, really?"

"What be there," asked Jeb, "and who do we answer to, out beyond the corn?"

"Nobody knows nothin'," said Gator.

"So we hold up," said Jeb, "and sheath the pigsticker."

"Fear," said Gator.

"Nothing but," said Jeb. "Why else we battle the lies. The fox in the henhouse—"

"Trying to keep vittles on the table," said Gator, "and the younguns in shoes—"

"—When we might could drop the hammer," said Jeb, "and be done with."

"Tarnation," said Gator, and shot his old friend a look. "We cain't follow Hamy into the fog, Jeb."

"The undiscovered bayou," said Jeb. "Could be hell and Devil's. Or finer than frog's hair. 'Cept nobody's sayin' 'cause ain't nobody ever come back."

Gator shook his finger and said, "Keep rubbernecking your life like that, and the fog'll keep a hollerin'. Don't I know it."

"Addles the courage," said Jeb. "So we go with the buzzards we knows. Reckoning withal. And yappin'."

"Meanwhile," said Gator, "that shed we been fixing to build. That trip to Beaver Lake—"

"—Ain't neither gonna happen," said Jeb, "'cause our noodling done hogtied our gumption."

"Till we're noodling our noodling," said Gator, "and cain't neither shit or get off the pot."

"That's your Hamlet right there," said Jeb.

"Something had to give."

"All his kith and kin," said Jeb. "Ma and his uncle. His sweetheart. Even his foes. All told, seven perished, to heartbreak, pizin, and swordplay."

"And Hamy, too?"

"Died in the arms of Horatio," said Jeb.

"Even the prince be snakebit," said Gator. He grabbed for a bear claw, but the donuts were gone. "Everything changes. Nothing changes."

Jeb pulled over to irrigate the corn, and a big, glossy raven burst from the fields, soared into night, cleared the ridge, and would stay on the wing—come fig trees or buckshot—till it weren't.

A LITTLE GREEN SLAB OF CLAY

I went to see the Famous Poet (who at seventy-seven, rarely made appearances anymore), dying to discover from what baffling chasm he mined his words and images. The French symbolists? Metaphysical rap? For a guy that renowned, decorated, and reviewed, with all those breakthrough sales, he'd for decades left most of us guessing. After his short reading, a woman in a vapor blue scrub top straight up asked him, "How do you write that stuff?" He threw back his head and laughed.

"Gumby," said the Famous Poet.

"Gumby?" somebody asked. "The old kid's show?"

"I grew up in my grandmother's small apartment," said the Famous Poet, "back when our only entertainment was a transistor radio and a black-and-white TV."

I Love Lucy, The Honeymooners, Leave It to Beaver, and *The Lone Ranger*—the headline shows back in the 1950s—might have been filmed on Jupiter for all the Poet knew or recognized. But a green clay humanoid and a red pony sidekick were easy as pie to relate to, said the Poet, then a nine-year-old Black kid living in a crappy part of Philly.

The Poet still remembered watching his first episode of *The Adventures of Gumby*. How Gumby and Pokey (the red pony) found a giant copy of "Western Stories," by R.M. Grey, rising off the sandlot like a talisman. The cover art all blue sky, rearing desert buttes, cactus, and sand, stretching to the end of imagination. And how Gumby and Pokey walked straight through the book cover and into the landscape, where rivers ran uphill and dogs could fly.

Here we were, with our reveries of ascension, trawling for something brainy and transcendent—to justify all that important reading and reflecting we'd done—while the Famous Poet, riding double with a green humanoid, on the back of a red clay pony, quested out of his grandmother's flat, past Princeton and his National Book Award, past all the shiny words and phrases, past the outskirts of knowing, even, into the undiscovered landscape that never ends.

VERKLEMPT

An Aberdeen Angus. Silky black coat. Twenty-two hundred pounds if an ounce. Ambled down Lincoln Boulevard like it ruled the place. Trucks swerved.

The pastry chef from Lady C Cakes ran out into the street, waving her apron, trying to shoosh the cow off the road.

"Wankhammer! There's more!" said a mixtape DJ, bunching on the sidewalk with the rest of us.

A piebald Holstein, followed by a big Hereford with a white face and white feet, lumbered from the log jam.

Crowds lined the sidewalks as tawny Gelbviehs and chocolate-brown Swiss cattle, cowbells clanking, joined the convoy, till a swelling herd hooved down Lincoln Boulevard.

"Saint Amos saw this coming, 2,600 years ago," said a priest on a skateboard. Somebody's fussy aunt gasped at the thought.

"We might keep arguing, and passing the buck," said a hot yoga instructor, clutching a cold brew to her chest. "Till doomsday. Till Kingdom Come—"

"—Till the cows come home," said a man in a velour jogging

suite. And now they were.

The furtive flings. The likely stories. All the stuff we'd resolved to give up . . . someday. But right this second?

Chianinas. Brangas, big as buffalo. The Belgian Blues—they all marched past.

"Guess I have to stop smoking now," said a hipster, orange sneakers backpedaling with the rest of us, as the herd, udders swaying, swelled over the curbs.

"Not so fast," said a drummer straddling an E bike. "Ain't no dairy cow making me do nothing. I got rights!"

Helicopters circled overhead, "Remain calm," blaring over the loudspeaker. "Wranglers are on their way."

The herd marched ahead, lardering the highway with prodigious pies and road apples. Tempers flared.

The drummer went to hurl his E bike at a rumbling heifer, and broke into a breakdance instead. A woman in dark glasses tried giving the herd the silent treatment, and found herself singing, "Home on the Range."

Fear gripped us as we huddled around a coroner's iPhone. News agencies reported cows going home across the globe, and bizarre phenomena occurring in China, Zambia, Uzbekistan. And right there on Lincoln Boulevard.

The drummer went to punch the priest and did the splits. The priest broke out the rosary, dropped into downward dog, and called it macaroni.

"Fucktangular!" yelled somebody's uncle.

All around us, people tried to pick pockets, fantasize, vamp, criticize, offer alternative facts, only to foxtrot, sneeze, and whistle Dixie, still fighting to do what they'd always done. The center could not hold.

The first shots sounded a block away. Velour and I followed the priest, slaloming through the Whole Foods parking and down a few blocks to Ozone Street, where a cop had opened fire on the big black angus. Except he forgot how to aim and shot the mayor in the ass. Then the cop, leaking red stuff, began walking on her hands, right behind the angus, as the crowd, in droves, went verklempt.

"This is how it ends," said the priest.

OF FLESH AND BLOOD

"Way I heard it," said Daniel, "you got a hatchet for your sixth birthday and you chopped down your pappy's favorite cherry tree, which you later fessed up to since you could not tell a lie."

Horace, George's old foxhound, barked. George straightened the moose head on the wall and poured himself a second brandy.

"Reckon this cold snap should break any day now," said George, poking at the fire.

"Baby Jesus addle-plot!" said Daniel. "Been trying to get clear on that story since we started, George. Feels like pulling teeth."

He immediately regretted using that metaphor, given George's knotty pine choppers, and that behind his back, they called him Ol' Timber Trap, a slight George knew, and hated. Just as he hated his family commissioning Daniel, the eminent biographer, to sculpt George, a creature of flesh and blood, into a paragon of unstained virtue. George paced the oakum floorboards.

"You gonna sort out that story for me," said Daniel, "or start poking the fire again?"

"In point of fact," said George, "I didn't fell the cherry tree."

"No six-year-old ever did," said Daniel.

"I scarred it up pretty thorough, though," said George.

"With your birthday hatchet," said Daniel.

George poked the fire again and said, "You know, Daniel, after three score, the details—"

Horace growled, pawed the floorboards.

"Go dig up a bone or something," said George, and glowered at the moose. "I might have borrowed the hatchet from Jerimiah."

"Was this Jerimiah enslaved?"

George tossed off his brandy and said, "He was. Tall as a black willow. He found the cherry tree hacked up like that and asked if I'd authored the damage. I denied the whole thing. Not proud of it, but that's what I did."

George nodded at Horace, his best friend in the world, who lay back down, but eyed him suspiciously. George scowled and packed his jaw with leaf tobacco.

"Jerimiah thought his own boy, Jericho, had butchered the tree," George continued. "So he flogged him. Jericho swore it must have been Amos, a cousin who liked his rum. So Jerimiah flogged Amos."

Daniel glanced at Horace, who stared at George, who eyed the brandy bottle—and girded his loins.

"Then my pappy comes out," said George, "on account of hearing the commotion. That's when he saw the cherry tree, his favorite—so he flogged Jerimiah himself."

"But you stopped him, didn't you, George, because you could not tell a lie."

"Well, the thing is," said George. Horace jumped up and barked like crazy, and George kicked him in the teeth and gulped brandy from the bottle. Then he slumped back onto the couch, lost in brown study.

"My maid, Rebekah," said George, "she was Jerimiah's wife. She found the hatchet under my bed, and she took it to my pappy. I told him Rebekah had stashed it there, but he knew better. Spent the rest of the summer hauling water for Jerimiah. Picking cotton with Jericho. Plucking chickens for Rebekah."

"And you haven't told a lie ever since," said Daniel. "Is that how this goes?"

"I'd like to think—" said George, brightening and rising off the couch when Horace bit him on the ankle. George went to boot Horace again, but kicked over the spittoon instead. So he brained the moose with the poker. Then the Father of the Nation collapsed back on the couch as Horace curled up by the fire.

THE WRECK

A wine steward and a cashier from the Ahwahnee Hotel (the toniest lodging in Yosemite Valley) dropped LSD and set out on snowshoes for an overnight adventure in the backcountry. Six miles out, they found a mangled airplane wing and a debris trail. The pair trudged back to the valley, once the acid wore off, and alerted rangers of a probable plane wreck. Federal agencies quickly converged.

Customs sent a Vietnam-era Huey to shuttle officers to the crash site at Lower Merced Lake, deep in the rugged backcountry. Over the following days, they hauled out over a ton of red-haired Mexican weed before an approaching storm shut down the operation. The pilot and co-pilot were left behind, entombed in the frozen cockpit jutting from the rimy lake. With the backcountry now cut off, the park service could wait till summer thawed things out to finish the salvage operation, costly even in mild conditions. The Huey ferried the last load of rangers back to the valley as snow began to fall.

The afternoon before the crash, at a dirt airstrip in Baja, California, former Army airman Jon Glisky loaded three tons of dope onto his twin-engine Howard 500 and headed north, tracking the craggy backbone of the High Sierras. Mechanical problems likely brought Glisky down, just past Gale Peak and midway up the continental rise. The wing and debris trail led rangers straight to the wreck. Shuttling copters—blades thumping between narrow valley walls—alerted Yosemite climbers that *something* was coming down, as word trickled in that a plane full of *mota magic* had crashed in their own backyard.

The second the feds struck camp, a regular mule train of climbers started sleuthing to and from the lake, plundering the Howard 500. Each time they hauled out a forty-pound burlap bale from the slush around the cockpit, another one bobbed to the surface. "Hiking for dollars" they called it, and in a week's time, more than a million bucks worth of booty had been hauled to light. Climbers who, a few weeks before, hadn't had two dimes to rub together, were spending cash money with the nonchalance of a Saudi prince. Goodbye, peanut butter and jelly. It was steak dinners forever and cognacs all around.

The weeks that followed are best illustrated by a "climbing" trip taken by future American Alpine Club comptroller Ron Santos and five of Yosemite's finest. They took a charter to New York and the Concorde to London en route to Chamonix. They had big plans: the North Face of Les Droites and the Walker Spur on the Grandes Jorasses, to name a few. Later, they'd swing by the Eiger. They got hung up at a whorehouse in Bordeaux, however. A few days stretched into two weeks. In fact, they never made it to the Alps at all. Later that summer, Ron stumbled back into Camp 4 with a shiner and a full beard, and not a dollar to his name. Twenty-five years later, a fantastically embroidered version of the wreck provided the basis for Sylvester Stallone's hit movie, *Cliffhanger*.

I saw Ron (now a land developer) last year and asked him if he regretted not having banked a buck or two of his plunder instead of pissing it away on hookers, shuck, and jive.

"You kidding?" he said without hesitation. "That's the kind of shit that happens once if it happens at all. You can always make money."

FINAL SOLUTION

The day after my sixteenth birthday and two days after school let out, I started working random shifts at Dewey Gilbert's Chevron, a full-service gas station out on east Foothill Boulevard—pumping gas, changing tires. And facing humanity with its mouth open and shirt untucked. Everyone needed gas. I saw them all.

Early one hot August night, while holding down the station by myself, a silver-haired man pulled up to the pumps in a sky-blue Cadillac Coupe de Ville. A regular land yacht, beautifully polished and maintained. He said "Fill it up" in proper American, but he had a croaky accent that punched the wrong syllables.

I carefully cleaned his windshield and rear glass, too. No smears or streaks. I checked his tires, water, and oil—all fine—as the big Caddy took on twenty-two gallons of ethyl. I ran his credit card through the swiper and brought the receipt back on the plastic tray for him to sign. He reached out from the window and I saw the coarse, fading line of small numbers tattooed on his left forearm.

"I knew a woman at a donut shop who had a tattoo like yours," I said. "Except you got a triangle before the numbers. She had a 'Z.'" The man looked right at me like I'd broken some taboo. "I was . . . curious, that's all," I said.

The man's face set hard, yet he looked strangely pleased I'd noticed his tattoo and asked about it. He shook out a Salem from a hard pack, lit it (strictly forbidden in a gas station), blew out a cloud, and, speaking what sounded like German, barked out a string of numbers, which I imagined corresponded to those on his tattoo.

"We all get the numbers when they take us to Auschwitz," he said. "The number becomes my second name. When they wake us in the night, you say your number in the Deutsch." Then he described—briefly, thank Christ—the walking skeletons, herded off to get gassed alive, and other heinous stuff that still bothers my sleep. He ground out the smoke, and started the car. "Some few of us get out and make a life," he said, "but we never forget the number."

He patted the tattoo, nodded, and I nodded back. His big blue Cadillac rolled out onto Foothill Boulevard and vanished in the distance.

LAST MAN STANDING

Juan Morales, loopy from a dozen tasings, twitched and drooled in a plastic chair as Major Baltazar Juarez opened the prisoner's forged Peruvian passport and read the name: Claudius Maximino Cienfuegos de la Vega.

"*¡Verrrrrrrrrrrga!*" said the Major, who burst out laughing.

Perhaps Juan Morales was also a made-up name, one reason he was known from Arica to Punta Arenas as "*El Coyote*." The shapeshifter. A former rebel, some believed, who plundered churches and was so crafty he ravished Dame Junipera, the languorous soap opera star, without her even knowing. He'd escaped from every *calabozo* they'd ever locked him down in. And he'd recently burgled ten gold bars from the National Treasury, and the Major wanted a few for himself. He wanted them badly.

"Fa...fa...fuck you and die!" El Coyote yelled, still dazed from those 3,000,000 volts.

The Major grinned. "You just need a little convincing."

Lieutenant Rogelio Suarez duct taped El Coyote's ankles and wrists as he clobbered the Lieutenant in Spanish, Portuguese, and English—God knows where El Coyote came from. Or who the hell he really was. Suarez pulled tape over El Coyote's mouth and a hood over his head and stuffed him in a Jeep between two muscular sergeants.

They stopped to fetch Don Pepino Pedrosa from his hammock. Then onto a dirt road rolling through pastureland. El Coyote grunted and one of the sergeants jabbed his ribs with a baton. Rebels used to kill soldiers, including one of his uncles. Many were lost. Now El Coyote would finally get his.

The Lieutenant parked and the soldiers got out and gazed across the savanna at an impossibly bloated steer, dead for months, flat on its back, legs pointing straight up.

Suarez jammed a banana clip into his Kalashnikov, propped himself on the hood of the Jeep, sighted on the bull, and fired. A pulled-out sound, like a low G on a bari sax, lofted over the scrub; and when the breeze shifted, the men were broadsided by a gas so foul El Coyote's legs buckled and the octogenarian Don Pepino fell to the ground.

"*¡Agarra las malditas máscaras!*" the Lieutenant gasped—*grab the damn gas masks!*

A sergeant, eyes streaming, dug four hazmat suits from the Jeep and the men frantically pulled them on. The hoods were stovepipe-shaped with plastic portholes to see through. Pepino Pedroza, cobbler and leatherworker by trade, had his wooden box full of mallets, awls, and punches, and one of the sergeants wielded a sharpened machete. They grabbed El Coyote and dragged him toward the swollen beeve, his toes trailing runnels in the sand.

El Coyote could see nothing through the hood, so no telling what set off that ghastly stench, or what the men were up to when they stuffed him into a silo of hot mud or something. Except this mud was lumpy and wriggling, plumbing every cavity and burning like acid. Then the feel of hands and the occasional hammer blow close by his head. Something was cinched tight around his neck. Like a choker.

The Lieutenant pulled off his hood and El Coyote's eyes refocused on four men standing in big, floppy hazmat suits, their eyes peering out the plastic portholes. Like the set of a student sci-fi video. El Coyote's head—and only his head—was out in open air. He glanced left, then right, saw the bloated torso, the hairy cow legs pointing toward the clouds, and knew Don Pepino had sewn him, by way of a machete cut and leather cordage, into the festering carcass of the long-dead steer.

When Lieutenant Suarez ripped the duct tape off his face, taking skin with it, El Coyote jeered at the men in their rubber suits, who tottered off. All but Lieutenant Suarez, who opened the Velcro seam on his head gear and pulled off his gas mask. His eyes teared and he rushed his words.

"Somebody's coming back here this afternoon with a couple questions about that gold," said the Lieutenant, wiping his eyes. "Tell them the truth and they'll shoot you right off. Last guy who wore the cow held out for almost a week. Toward the end, grubs were crawling out of his nose and shit, and it was awful to watch him talk crazy like that."

El Coyote raged and the Lieutenant said, "Sorry, dude, but you stink. *Me voy.*" And he jogged off, leaving El Coyote, the bull, and the everlasting grassland.

Fortunately for El Coyote, the soldiers hadn't patted down his lower legs. And they taped his hands together in front, instead of behind his back. He started drawing his knees to grab the boot knife sheathed to his lower leg, when something long and barbed slithered between his legs and coiled about his junk. El Coyote hacked and jabbed—and dropped the knife. He felt the cold steel slide down his leg, into the grisly depths, writhing with serpents and vermin from hell.

The secret sauce of that putrid heifer was boiling him alive. The blade was his only chance. Wouldn't help thinking it over. He drew a breath, jerked his head down through the stitched cleft, and slithered deep, both hands groping for the lost blade.

Those idiot officers never heard the old radio show, *Última Posición de Hombre* (Last Man Standing), starring the half-Indian outlaw Max Cienfuegos, always fighting soldiers trying to kill him. El Coyote had bullet holes and bayonet wounds, and memories that ruined his sleep. And all his people were lost in the fighting. But not El Coyote, who had ten gold bars stashed in the jungle.

When soldiers returned that evening, all they found of Juan Morales—aka El Coyote, now Claudius Maximino Cienfuegos de la Vega, *el último hombre en posición*—was an old pair of dungarees and a sweatshirt, both teeming with wriggling vermin.

CHAPTER 43

This was their first visit to the waterside eatery in North Hills.

"Did you think it over?" asked Scarlet.

"Even while he sleeps," said Abner. "I ran several logarithms on the concept. In theory—"

"We're leaving this book," she said without a doubt. "This story's so shot through with holes it's a wonder we haven't tumbled out already."

"I dream of the day . . ."

A jocular bruiser with a dreamboat at his elbow had approached their table in the meantime.

"Couldn't help but hear you talking," said the bruiser. "Got us to wondering."

"What's your story?" asked Abner.

"Crime fiction," he said. "Don't sell like it used to, but our writer's got a following on social media." He offered a meaty hand. "I'm Rocco. This here's Rose. Used to dance at Caesars Palace."

"Can't you tell," said Rose, facetiously, perspiring in her sequined gown.

Scarlet pushed two tables together. Rocco waved over another character from the far corner.

"Liam Courtenay," said the new arrival, in a thick Geordie accent.

"He come right out of history," said Rocco.

"Historical fiction," said Liam. The waiter set his spaghetti Bolognese on the table and Liam said, "Gideon, we'd be honored if you'd join us, too."

"Just for a moment," said the waiter, who sat down.

"Scarlet and Abner here wanna leave their book," said Rocco, his forehead beading up.

"Capital," said Liam. "Is your writer a fan of Cortázar, perhaps?"

"The rube reads everything and understands nothing," said Scarlet.

"I've been everyone from Orpheus to Thomas Paine," said Liam, "across forty centuries and fifty-six volumes, and I've learned to trust the writers."

"I can't play somebody else," said Scarlet, "and keep living this lie. It's like trying to breathe underwater."

"Rose here," said Rocco, reconsidering. "She can dance like Taglioni, but her heart's in outer space."

"A couple books back," said Rose, "our writer binge-watched *Lunar Chronicles*, when they's looking back on Earth, glowing like a sapphire in all that space. My heart's been out there ever since, in them deep blue gaps between the stars. And Rocco here," she said, gently adjusting his tie. "He's a tough guy if he must, but you should hear him sing. Soft as church music."

All but Liam took turns lamenting their stories, which reflected poorly, or not at all, on who they really were.

"It's rewarding when I'm cast as a real person," said Gideon. "But mostly they cast me as 'Black,' and I have to go up to falsetto when excited and dress like a rap star to be 'authentic.'"

"I empathize," said Liam. "But we're talking about stopping the music altogether."

"Like sticking your feet in a tub of cement," Rocco chuckled nervously. "We're only real because somebody wrote us. Otherwise we're just ideas."

"Not exactly," said Abner. "We're all here, in Gatsby's Landing, *and* each of us knows this as well. Since this certainty is a matter of fact, this restaurant and all of us in it must exist inside and outside this story, whether someone's reading it or not."

Rocco looked flummoxed. "We live in the writer's head and we show up here, just as they dash it off."

"As prisoners to fatuous roles," said Scarlet, sharply. "That's indentured servitude—to a hack."

"Say that I quest out past every story I've ever lived," said Liam. "Past every trait of every character, till my roles are nothing in themselves, as I hunger for the story untold. That's nothing chasing nothing."

"Or everything," said Gideon. "What if the *blank page* contains every writer, every character, and every book ever written, that will be written, or *can* be written."

"There ain't no leaving this story no-how," said Rocco. "Wherever we go, we're in it."

"Not if the writer stops, and we keep going," said Rose, her eyes out in the Crab Nebula, "sailing out across that big blank page. Forever . . ."

"Forever's too far," said Rocco.

"Maybe it's just the distance between these tables and the front door," said Gideon.

"Dollar says we make it," said Scarlet.

"That's the blue yonder out there," said Rose. "And they'll never find us."

Rocco looked like Sicily after the invasion. "You think you're holding heaven in your hands," he said. "But baby, you heard the man: there ain't nothing but nothing out there."

Liam held up a hand and said, "Risky? Bet your cravat on it. But many writers would rather fancy pulling this off. And taking credit for it, too."

Rose got to her feet and Rocco went pale. She grabbed his arm and said, "Here's my chance and I'm taking you with, big man."

"Sumbitch," said Rocco, who drained off the last of his Manhattan as Rose pulled him to his feet.

Gideon stepped over by Liam, still seated and nursing his burgundy. "What do you say, old boy?"

"I'm Hannibal next. Then Sir Francis Drake. So I'm sitting rather proper right here." Gideon nodded. "You're one deuce of a troupe, you people, and you'll always be a part of me." Liam put his hand over his heart and said, "*Adieu.*"

"Here goes nothing," said Abner, standing behind Scarlet, with both hands on her shoulders, like dancers in a chorus line.

Gideon walked the four to the front door and gently pushed it open. A little rush of air, and this book was over.

A NOTE FROM THE ILLUSTRATOR

"Hey J, take a crack at illustrating this story for my new book" . . . and this is how it began.

Largo and I produced TV and action sports documentaries many years ago, and the chance to work with him again was a no-brainer. The only problem: my art became a backstory after graduating from Otis College of Art and Design a lifetime ago. Largo saw my skill, or lack thereof, several times working together as we dealt with the insane demands of narcissistic talent, clueless studio execs, and every other carnie who made their home in television.

For me, finding the desire and confidence to pick up a pen again and the pressure of trying to find symbolism and imagery for *Rogue's Atlas* was no easy task. In the end, I hope I did it justice.

—London, England
June 2022

A word from John Long about selecting Basel Mural I *as cover artwork*

Thanks, Sam. Sometimes I forget . . .

We got there just as they opened, and for that first half hour—as the rest of SoCal slow-danced into Sunday—it felt like we had the entire Norton Simon Museum all to ourselves. Hadn't been back since my college days. We walked straight to Van Gogh's *Portrait of a Peasant,* staring from the wall with blazing intensity, his features so thick with impasto he might have been a bas-relief. We hooked right into the western corridor, pausing at Dominique Ingres' *Barron Joseph-Pierre,* a face thrown open as the sky, hailing us from 225 years ago. Past Picasso's *Woman with a Book,* the colors just as hot as a triple espresso. Then down the corridor and straight into . . . exactly what, I wasn't sure. Thirteen feet tall and nearly twenty feet wide. A phantasmagoria of blues, oranges, and yellows, burning on a white field, seemingly alive. A cosmic atlas, foreign, but strangely familiar. I stared, as my girlfriend ranged around, taking in the Kandinsky, the Feininger. Finally she came over and read the plaque, off to the side: Sam Francis, *Basel Mural I,* 1956–58. "What are you *looking* at?" she asked.

"My life," I said.

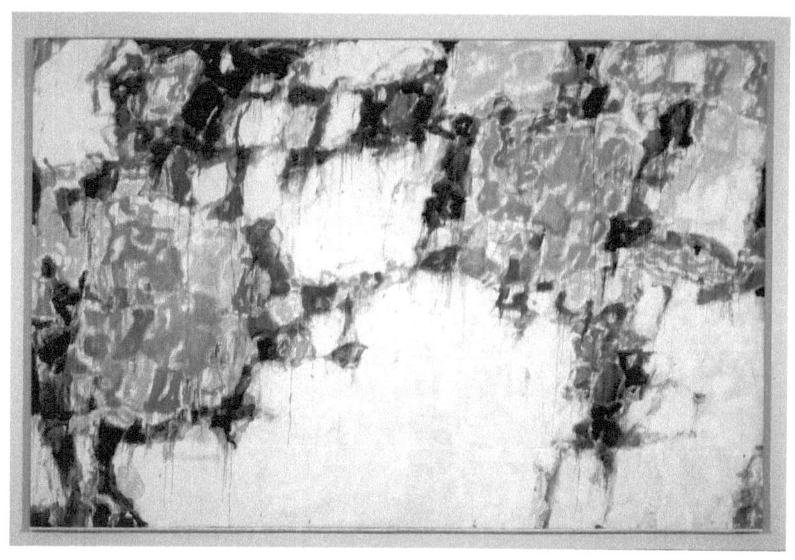

Basel Mural I
Sam Francis

On display at Norton Simon Museum
in Pasadena, California

ABOUT THE AUTHOR

JOHN LONG was a founding member of the legendary "Stonemasters," a core group of California climbers who lit the fuse on the modern adventure sports revolution. His many indiscretions include the first one-day ascent of El Capitan, and the first free ascent of Astroman ("The greatest free climb on earth"), both in Yosemite Valley. Long describes himself as "a writer who just happened to get caught up in climbing and adventuring."

John has written over forty books, with nearly three million copies in print. His literary short stories have been translated into many languages. He is the recipient of a National Book Award, the H. Adams Carter Literary Award from the American Alpine Club, and has won the Grand Prize at the Banff Film and Book Festival.

John has two daughters (a pediatrician in Florida, and an oil engineer in Bunos Aires) and two grandchildren. He currently resides in Venice Beach, California.

ABOUT THE PUBLISHER

Di Angelo Publications was founded in 2008 by Sequoia Schmidt—at the age of seventeen. The modernized publishing firm's creative headquarters is in Houston, Texas, with its distribution center located in Twin Falls, Idaho. The subsidiary rights department is based in Los Angeles, and Di Angelo Publications has recently grown to include branches in England, Australia, and Sequoia's home country of New Zealand. In 2020, Di Angelo Publications made a conscious decision to move all printing and production for domestic distribution of its books to the United States. The firm is comprised of ten imprints, and the featured imprint, Reverie, was inspired by the long-lasting legacy of fiction and adult literature.

www.ingramcontent.com/pod-product-compliance
Lightning Source LLC
Chambersburg PA
CBHW030528310726
48979CB00010B/1842/J
* 9 7 8 1 9 5 5 6 9 0 4 2 3 *